D1323770

SLEEPER

ABOUT THE AUTHOR

J.D. Fennell was born in Belfast at the start of the Troubles, and began writing stories at a young age to help understand the madness unfolding around him. Also a lover of reading he devoured a diverse range of books - his early influences include Fleming, Tolkein, Shakespeare and the Brontës.

He left Belfast at the age of nineteen and worked as a chef, bartender, waiter and later began a career in writing for the software industry.

These days he divides his time between London and Brighton, where he lives with his partner and their two dogs.

Sleeper

J.D. Fennell

THE
DOME
PRESS

Published by The Dome Press, 2017

A CIP catalogue record for this book is available from the British Library

ISBN 978-0-995-67233-8

The Dome Press
23 Cecil Court
London WC2N 4EZ

www.thedomepress.com

Printed and bound in Great Britain by Clays, St. Ives PLC
Typeset using Atomik ePublisher from Easypress Technologies

MIX
Paper from
responsible sources
FSC® C018072

For my beautiful Mum
Forever loved
Forever missed

Chapter 1

Deception

Many must die for the world to change.

Will bristles at Colonel Frost's parting words as he pushes his bicycle along the gloomy path through the woods. He pulls at the stiff, starched collar of his gleaming white shirt giving passage to a bead of cold sweat that rolls from his nape and scurries down his spine. He shudders and tries not to think about Frost and his men who follow in the woods on either side. Armed, and invisible in the darkness, they watch his every move. His heart pounds like a hammer and he wonders if they can feel it vibrating through the trees. He swallows. Despite his nerves, his excitement for this mission is at tipping point. So too is his anticipation for the twist that he is about to stir into the pot – a twist that would result in his torture and execution. If Frost catches him, that is. He would not let that happen. There was too much at stake for it all to go wrong now.

"You are one of us, Will," Frost had said. "Four years I have overseen your training and I could not be prouder. Today will be your baptism of blood. Do not fail me. Do not fail our masters."

Masters! Will had almost baulked at that. His hands curl into fists at the thought. He had held his tongue, his expression fixed, his face a mask, a mask he had worn since this all began just over four years back. To this day it still surprises him how he has managed to hide the truth of who he is from Frost. But then again, anything is possible when the desire for retribution runs this deep.

He shifts uncomfortably in the clothes Frost made him wear. Expensive as they are, they feel a little snug compared to the rough military fatigues he has worn every day for the past four years. Four years. The time had passed so slowly yet it only seems like yesterday when he became one of *them*.

He loosens his tie, undoes the top button and breathes in.

That's better.

He is sixteen, with dark hair and is well built for his age. The schoolboy image does not sit well with him. It reminds him of another time, when he was someone else.

Someone normal.

The stirring of old memories makes him tremble inside; he closes his eyes, takes three breaths and carefully pushes the thoughts from his mind.

'Another time,' he whispers and recalls Frost's orders: 'Remember what you are, what you are capable of. The school uniform is a disguise. It will make you seem less of a threat,' he had said. Loath as Will was to admit it, Frost was right.

He stops when he hears the approaching drone of a Spitfire patrol. The air vibrates, the trees sway and rustle as the fighters storm overhead flying south over Hastings. A squadron to intercept random raids from German fighters, he guesses.

Emerging from the trees he hears a swing band and laughter coming from a house beyond the vast wall. He sees two guards standing by a pair of tall iron gates watching the Spitfires disappear into the night. With a light tread, he approaches and coughs politely. The men jump and spin around with pistols pointing directly at Will.

'Hello,' says Will in a friendly tone.

'Stop right there,' says the guard on the left as he removes something from his pocket with his free hand. A torch.

A dim light sweeps Will's face and body.

'Ha, it's just a schoolboy,' mocks the guard.

'He looks a bit old for that uniform,' says the other.

Will smiles and steps forward, 'Excuse me…'

'I said, stay right there!'

Will ignores him. 'Please, I'm afraid my bicycle has a flat tyre. Do you mind if I use your telephone? I must call my father. He'll be terribly worried.'

'Clear off, boy,' says the other guard.

Will's mouth dries, but he cracks a sweet smile.

The guards look at each other, laugh and pocket their weapons.

Will seizes his moment and swings the bicycle at the guard on the left, who drops the torch and falls backward slamming his temple on the gate pillar. He slumps to the ground unconscious. Before the second guard can pull out his weapon, Will is on him, his fist slamming into his jaw in a fierce blow. The guard is out cold before his hand reaches his gun.

'I am no schoolboy.'

He crushes the torch with his foot, killing the light, and glances behind him, aware that Frost and the agents of VIPER are watching. He swallows hard, trying his best not to give himself away. Four years of hard training, all of it leading up to this moment, this sweet deception.

Dragging the guards away from the path, he removes the Welrod silencer pistol from his satchel. He stands where he knows Frost can see him, points the pistol toward the men and shoots.

He hurries toward the manor house, darting between the bushes that line the drive. He hears water trickling and stops, his foot cracking a twig. A confused face appears from behind a tree. A guard relieving himself. Their eyes lock. The guard shouts out and fumbles for his gun, but Will slams the man's head against the rough bark and let's him fall forward into his urine.

Rapid footsteps crunch on gravel. The fourth guard. Will dips behind the tree and pulls a small tube, the length of a pencil, from the inner sleeve of his blazer. He locates a row of small darts beneath his collar, removes two and slips one into a rest inside the tube. He hears a pistol cocking as the footsteps become slow and cautious on the grass near the tree. His assailant's breathing is fast, making his location easy to determine.

Will slides around the trunk and shoots a dart at the guard. The man stiffens as he grabs his neck, his face contorting as the poison works fast and renders him temporarily paralysed.

Will pops the second dart into the pipe and slips it back into his sleeve. No one from the party will have seen or heard what is happening outside. The music is loud and the windows are draped with heavy blackout curtains and anti-blast tape.

'Every cloud…' he whispers.

The party will be in full swing. He imagines revellers dressed in dinner suits and cocktail dresses drinking champagne and dancing as if they don't care that there is a war on and the world is in crisis. He wonders if the Grandmaster and his henchman, the Pastor, are present. He is the one person he fears the most: Gideon the Pastor, or the holy man as some people call him, an innocuous title for a monster of a man. Will shivers at the thought of the bloody stories he has heard about him. But there is no time to think about those now.

He circles out of sight to the side entrance, removes a lock pick from his inside sleeve, picks the lock and cautiously opens the door. The reception hall is dimly lit with a scattering of candles and the smell of alcohol and smoke lingers in the air. The space is vast and ornate, but in an old style, as if it is somehow stuck in time. Crossing to the drawing room, he freezes, thinking he sees a shadow flit across the landing. Could it be that not everyone is at the party? He squints, but sees no one. A trick of the light, or a symptom of nerves, perhaps.

Reaching into his satchel, he removes three round metal balls, each the size of a fist. He presses a button on each one. They make a ticking sound, a countdown of ten seconds before the ether gas will be released. He opens the drawing-room door and rolls them along the floor towards the party-goers and the band.

The balls pop and hiss loudly as he closes the door.

And then the music stops, he hears bodies fall to the floor and glass smash on the hardwood. Someone tries to leave the room, a fist bangs weakly on the door, but Will holds it tight. A moment later, all is quiet. The party is over.

His mission is to find the notebook and spare no lives. But Will has other plans. The notebook is in the library on the first floor, locked in the Grandmaster's safe. He hurries up the stairs, glances around, recalling the layout from this morning's final briefing.

'Hello,' says a flat emotionless voice.

Will jumps, his heart thumping. Emerging from the shadows is a tall thin man with long white hair brushed back from his head. His eyes are small, like coals buried in two deep pits. A small tongue darts out and dampens his thin lips, as if he is hungry. His suit is black, like a preacher's.

Will's spine goes cold. It is Gideon, the Pastor.

'I'm afraid the Grandmaster has retired for the evening,' says the Pastor as he cocks his ear to the side. His eyes narrow as he registers that the party has gone quiet.

Something shiny opens in his hand. A razor.

Will swallows, faltering for a moment, trying desperately not to think of the horror stories he has heard about this vile man's reputation. He feels beads of perspiration prickling like frantic ants on his forehead.

'Who are you?' asks Gideon.

Will has to act. Deftly, his fingers reach into his sleeve for the pipe, but the holy man's eyes flare and he runs at Will, the razor raised in the air ready to cut. Will is fast. He blows the dart at Gideon, whose attempt to deflect it leaves it lodged in the inside of his wrist. He grimaces and groans, his gnarly fingers stiffening as the poison seeps through his body.

Will trembles, the razor is inches from his face. He steps back as the Pastor falls to the floor, his eyes mad with fury at this indignity. Will edges around him, conscious that time is not on his side.

'Gideon, what is that noise?' comes a voice.

Will looks up to see the Fellowship's Grandmaster emerge from the library. He is old and decrepit, his blue eyes watery and confused.

Will removes the pistol from the satchel and points it at the old man. 'Inside,' he commands.

'What have you done?' asks the Grandmaster.

'Nothing to worry about. Your henchman is incapacitated for a short period.'

The Grandmaster retreats into the library. 'What do you think you are doing? My men…'

'Shut up,' Will snaps. 'They are unharmed. Your men and your guests are out of action for the moment.'

Will glances around the room. There is a portrait on a wall. If Frost is right, the notebook is stored behind the painting. He points the pistol at it. 'Open it. Give me the book.'

The old man pales.

'I don't know what you are talking about.'

Will glances through the curtains at the grounds and beyond the wall. It is only a matter of time before Frost figures out something is not quite right.

'We have no time. In moments the agents of VIPER will storm this house and kill all of you. There is a chance you will survive, if you do what I say.'

The old man sneers and scoffs. 'You're just a boy. What do you know about anything?'

Will's eyes blaze. He grabs the Grandmaster's wrist and drags him to the portrait with the barrel of his pistol lodged in the crook of the old man's neck. Will twists his arm and watches as his face contorts with pain, his eyes staring into Will's. What has he become? What have VIPER turned him into? But he has no time for morality now. There is too much at stake.

'Open the safe.'

He presses the barrel deeper into the Grandmaster's neck. The old man struggles for breath and coughs, his face burning red. Trembling, he lifts his hands and concedes.

He opens the safe.

Will sees a small book-size parcel inside, wrapped in an aged oilskin cloth. His mouth dries and he hesitates before slipping it into the satchel and backing out of the room.

'You can't do this,' says the Grandmaster. 'You don't know what you are dealing with.'

'Better that I have this, than VIPER. I suggest you hide somewhere. They will be here any minute. With me gone they may not waste time killing you and your guests as they hunt for me. But that is something that I cannot guarantee.' He turns and hurries out of the library, skipping carefully over the twisted form of the paralysed holy man.

'You won't get far. Gideon will find you. I can promise you that.'

The Grandmaster's words send a chill over Will. He bolts down the stairs with a grim feeling that he should have finished Gideon off for good.

Chapter 2

Escape

Will scurries along the shadows of the perimeter wall, with the parcel tucked safely into his satchel. He had done it! He had seized the notebook. The plan had unfolded as Frost had predicted, with the exception of Will's modifications: the ether bombs and the pretence of killing the guards. Why should any more innocent people die? There was a war on and enough people were dying already. He had handled the notebook with tentative revulsion as if it was infected with some sort of disease. But it is worse than that. He knows what destruction its secrets could bring in the hands of VIPER. His only thought now is to get it far away from Frost and his ruthless pack of killers.

Looking back at the house, he imagines Frost's men searching the rooms. On the ground floor the Colonel will be prowling, surveying Will's handiwork. He will be furious. A smirk cracks on Will's face at the thought. He hates Frost; he hates them all for what they have done.

The two guards are stirring as he slips through the gates and sprints towards the woods. The blast of a gunshot shatters the silence. Frost's men, his former colleagues, have spotted him. He ducks as something whizzes past his ear and splinters the bark of a tree directly in front of him. Glancing back, he sees the Fellowship's guards are up and searching for their weapons, too. Will hears the booming voice of the Colonel barking an order. It is cut off sharply by the crack of pistols. Will takes cover and catches his breath.

More gunfire erupts. He recognises the short recoil of the pack's Johnson semi-automatic rifles. The guards do not stand a chance. Will hopes they have the sense to clear out. A chase might keep some of the agents of VIPER off his tail.

With his heart racing, he hurries blindly through the woods, ignoring the twigs that lash out at his face and body. The area is unfamiliar and the terrain uneven, causing him to stumble twice. The gunfire has ceased and Will wonders what has become of the guards. Have they been gunned down mercilessly like so many others?

Behind him, he hears howling, the signal that Frost and his pack are hunting. This time, Will is their prey.

He runs.

His blood thunders in his ears and sweat cools on his face as he reaches the edge of the trees and clears the woods. The sky is an inky black canopy with a scattering of stars and a thin waxing crescent moon that provides a small measure of silvery light. He can see the narrow country road where they parked the cars earlier. They are somewhere here, but where?

The howling is getting closer.

He sees beams of torchlight scanning the woods. With the sleeve of his blazer, he wipes the sweat from his brow and glances up and down the road. He spots a line of bushes almost twenty yards ahead. They seem out of place, as if they had just been propped there. He hurries towards them and sees a glimpse of something gleaming behind them. There!

Torch beams slice through the darkness. Frost is reckless, believing himself and VIPER above the law. They care nothing for wartime blackout rules and he would gladly put a bullet into heart of a local bobby or the Home Guard if they were unlucky enough to challenge him.

As Will moves towards the cars, he wonders what will be his fate if he doesn't manage to escape. Inevitably he would die, but not quickly. Before death there would be torture, questions bellowed into his ears: Who are you? Why did you do it? Who are you working for? That was the million-dollar question. Who was he working for? Will was no longer so sure of that himself.

For four years he had lived learning to become one of them, at someone else's request. He had his own reason for doing it, of course: revenge. Frost had called him 'the boy with the fire in his belly', and he was not wrong. Will's desire for vengeance had made it easy for him to keep his mask up. He had fooled them all with the intention of destroying them. He had waited four years, living with these murderers, all the while being fed secret messages from Control. He had done his best and waited for the opportunity to infiltrate VIPER and bring them down, but that opportunity had never arisen. And then, out of the blue, Colonel Frost had given him his first mission. The agents of VIPER's most important mission: acquire the notebook containing the whereabouts of a weapon so powerful it could cause destruction on a massive scale. This was no ordinary weapon. It was something ancient and otherworldly. VIPER were experts in mixing science with the occult. Will had heard some strange stories and seen some weird things in his four years. If the stories about this weapon were true, he could not let VIPER have control of something so awful. Thousands would perish. *Many must die for the world to change.* That was VIPER's mantra. Will was sick to the stomach of hearing it. He could not allow that to happen. He had set aside his own personal vendetta in order to get the notebook away and figure out what to do with it. Give it to Control or destroy it himself. The details hadn't seemed important.

The cars are lined up in a row facing the road and hidden from view. There are three Austin 8s, a general-purpose model chosen by Frost. Anything more ostentatious might cause people to look twice and raise suspicion. From his satchel, Will takes out the car keys he had nimbly stolen from the pocket of one of the more careless soldiers. The howling draws closer; torchlight spills onto the road.

Having climbed into one of the Austins, he turns over the ignition. It coughs momentarily before springing into life. He breathes a sigh of relief. Despite the war, no expense is spared with VIPER. The best of everything is provided: food, accommodation, rewards, weapons and cars. They invested a lot and expected much in return. This was one moment when he could be grateful for their largesse.

Will steps on the accelerator and releases the handbrake. He spins the wheel and speeds up the country road as the pack emerges from the woods in one long line. They must have doubled their efforts to find him. Two are ahead of him, shining their torches at the Austin. Will raises his hand to his eyes to stave off the glare. He hears the rapid crack of the Johnson rifles. The car judders at the impact of the bullets, but he is unhurt. VIPER have invested well – the Austin, like all their vehicles, is bullet proof. Will glances in the rear-view mirror. His throat dries. He is not out of trouble yet. The pack are climbing into the remaining cars. He knows Frost will do everything in his power to stop him escaping. He has the notebook and he knows too much. Will grips the steering wheel, slams the accelerator and drives for his life.

Chapter 3

The End of the Road

Will swears under his breath. If only he'd had more time, he could have disabled the other cars. He focuses on the dark narrow road ahead and recalls the route he memorised at this morning's briefing. He knows Hastings town is nearby, and with it the possibility of finding a telephone box. All he has to do is call the operator and quote the four-digit number. He would be put through to Control and, after he gave him the code, Control would advise him what to do. He just had to find a telephone box.

Behind him the road is lit up with the beams from the headlights of the two Austins. This part of his plan makes him the most nervous. It has been three months since he passed his Driving Proficiency test. He can handle a car, but has little experience on the roads, unlike his murderous ex-colleagues who are adults with many years driving experience behind them. It is entirely possible they will catch up with him. And when they do, they will run him off the road headfirst into the nearest tree. But, the fate of humanity is inside Will's leather satchel. He has to think of something fast. Something they will not predict.

Up ahead, tall trees lined either side of the road, their branches stretching across and forming a natural tunnel. With his hands gripping the wheel Will plunges into what seems like a vacuum of darkness. He can see nothing and has no choice but to switch on the headlamps. He takes a breath and tries to get his bearings. If his memory is correct, there is a turning around the next corner, which leads to Hastings' ruins and the road down into the village. He considers his options: first find a telephone box and make contact with Control. The pack are right behind him. It will be easy to find a public telephone box but it would take a miracle for him to put through a call without getting a bullet in his back. First things first, he has to lose the agents of VIPER.

He speeds around a corner a little too fast and almost loses control of the car. The wheel slides through his damp palms as he fights to turn it. He gasps but manages to steady it in time. He glances in the rear-view mirror. The beams from the other cars are out of sight for the moment. Ahead he can see the right turn-off, so he eases the brakes and steers into it, the tyres crunching noisily on what is just a narrow gravel path. Switching off the headlamps he continues to drive waiting for his eyes to adjust to the gloom, praying that he doesn't hit a tree or drive off into a ditch.

He hears the other two Austins speeding by and breathes a sigh of relief. It will only take moments for them to realise he is not ahead of them, so he must hurry.

It is too dark. He has no choice but to turn the lights back on. The gravel path is getting steeper, and the terrain clearer. He looks to the road below and sees a car speeding along it. Considering how fast it is going, it could only be the pack. It turns up the gravel path. Will's heart sinks. He slams on the accelerator and wonders where the third car could be.

He is hot; the windows inside the car are steaming up. He winds down the driver's window, and tastes the air which is thick with salt. At the top of the gravel path there is no discernible road to follow. He can see the stone ruins of Hastings Castle and hear the surf lapping against the nearby cliffs, but he sees no one. Beyond the ruins is the village, and with it, the promise of a telephone box or even a new car he can steal.

Behind him, the second Austin is gaining ground. But where was the third? No time to worry about that now. He rubs the back of his neck. Think. Think. He wonders if he has any weapons left? With one hand on the wheel he opens the satchel and searches inside. He steadies his breathing and thinks hard. After a few seconds, he decides what he must do.

Will stops the car and gets out. He leans back inside, releases the brake and pushes the Austin back down the gravel path, watching with satisfaction as it hurtles toward the oncoming car containing one half of the pack. As much as he would love to watch the collision he has precious little time. He turns and sprints through the ruins of the castle. Behind him, he hears a satisfying crunch and the sound of the pack's voices shouting in alarm. An explosion follows. He smiles to himself and runs in the direction of the village.

And then, the blinding light of headlamps appears in the darkness, only twenty yards ahead. Will skids to a halt, squinting in the bright light. There is a broad figure silhouetted in the glare. A figure he knows well. Frost.

'Very impressive, William. I have taught you well.'

Will's heart pounds angrily in his chest. But he isn't afraid. He balls his fists. 'You're not getting the notebook, Colonel,' he says, clutching the satchel tightly.

The Colonel's eyes flick to the bag and back to Will. He is unarmed, but Will knows better than to feel secure about that. Behind the pack leader, the agents of VIPER wait, their rifles ready to riddle the betrayer with holes.

A horrible sense of loss sweeps over him and for a second it seems hopeless and that his elaborate plans has failed. But he is not one to give up so easily. He has already decided he would die trying, if that's what it takes.

'Give me the bag, William.'

Will reaches slowly into his bag, takes out the Welrod pistol and points it at the Colonel. In the darkness the rifles click in unison, ready to take out their target. Will's muscles coil.

The Colonel gestures to the pack. 'Lower your rifles.' He looks at Will and raises his arms. 'I am unarmed. It doesn't have to be this way. Just give me the bag.'

'No!' Will points the Welrod at Frost's chest.

'Why do this, William? You, of all people. I gave you a life. I gave you a purpose.'

Will's grip on the pistol tightens. 'You murdering bastard, you destroyed my life!'

'Ah. I see. I had no idea. Many must die for the world to change, William. That is our goal. It is what you signed up for.'

There is a hint of mockery in the Colonel's voice that makes Will's shoulders tighten but he steadies his breathing and focuses. The pack leader is baiting him.

'Give me the bag and we'll say nothing more of it.'

Will thinks quickly. Nothing would give him greater satisfaction than snuffing out this monster's lights. But there is still the remotest of chances he can win. He squeezes the trigger. His first shot hits the left headlamp. Swiftly, he points at the right headlamp and extinguishes the light, plunging them all into darkness.

The rifles fire as Will ducks and scrambles back toward the ruins, diving behind an ancient wall as a volley of bullets speeds in his direction. Tiny specs of stone spray his clammy face. Wiping them away, he catches his breath. What now? The gravel track may be his only option. He makes a dash towards it as more of the pack hurry towards the ruins. The village road would make him an open target. He turns towards the cliffs. Fast footfalls thunder on the ground near the ruins. He has no choice. He jumps from the ruins and sprints towards the darkness.

'There!' shouts a voice.

The rapid crack of gunfire fills the air as bullets fly past him and out to sea. He keeps running, praying one will not find his back. There is something up ahead. Eyes wide, he gasps and skids to a halt, inches from the edge of the cliff, staring down at an angry sea. If he had kept running he would have certainly fallen to his death. It is at least a 500-foot drop. He trembles, inching back slowly. Then, the beam of a torchlight sweeps behind him.

Will's heart ices over. As his eyes adjust to the torchlight, he can see the Colonel and, behind him, the pack.

'It's over William. Give me the bag.'

Will reaches into the bag.

'Just the bag.'

Will removes it from his shoulder and tosses it toward them. The pack leader gestures to the nearest soldier, who obediently picks it up.

'It's the end of the road. You understand I cannot let you live. My masters would not allow it and besides, my wolves need a kill. They need blood.'

Frost's men began howling in appreciation.

The Colonel smiles.

Suddenly, the pack's howling ceases and one by one they fall to the ground. Will watches with satisfaction as the pack leader looks about him in confusion. The Colonel sniffs the air taking in the scent of the ether bombs Will had set off in his bag. Fury fills his face as he covers his nose and mouth with his arm and stumbles forward. With his free hand he pulls out his Browning and levels it at Will.

Will tries to turn, but the Browning fires. Pain explodes in Will's chest and he stumbles backward, confusion filling his mind. His head slams against a rock and he feels himself weightless, upside down, falling, falling, falling. A bitter wind seems to cut right through him and then everything goes dark.

Chapter 4

Skipper

Will's eyes snap open as his body crashes through the hard surface of the water. Freezing cold envelopes him, numbing the pain in his chest and head, sucking him down, and spinning him in circles, deeper and deeper into an icy hell.

How…? Who…? What…?

His limbs thrash, trying desperately to swim to the surface but he is too tired. He sees nothing but perpetual darkness.

Breathe slowly… mustn't panic.

Exhaling through his nose, he relaxes his arms and legs in an effort to control his technique. He swims, but could be swimming downwards for all he knows. And then, he feels the pull as his body begins to float up. His eyes are sore with saltwater but above him there is the slither of the moon, hazy through a veil of choppy water.

He breaks the surface and gasps, sucking in every breath greedily. Waves slap his face and ears as he fights to tread water. A hot pain sears through his temple and a fierce freezing sensation penetrates his stomach as if he's been stabbed by a hundred icicles. His strength is diminishing; he feels his mind losing focus. He knows this is no nightmare and he won't wake up in a safe warm bed. He can't keep his eyes open. His mind empties into darkness.

And then he hears a voice calling, and with it the sound of chugging, getting closer and closer. He is completely numb now; his body seems detached from his head and all he wants to do is go to sleep. He feels peaceful, stops fighting, closes his eyes and sinks once more below the surface of the water. But then something hard and sharp pokes at his back and tugs at his clothes, pulling him upwards.

He dreams he is sprinting through the streets of London with a pack of vicious rabid dogs on his trail. He can see his house, but strangely it is boarded up as if no one lives there. He glances behind and sees the snarling beasts closing in, their yellow teeth bloody and soiled with strips of human flesh. With a burst of energy, he springs forward and opens the front door. Inside, the house seems empty and unloved as if no one has lived there for a long time. The rooms are thick with shadows, dust and cobwebs. He thinks this is not his house, yet it is so familiar.

'I'm... I'm home,' he calls, but no one answers.

He steps inside and notices the floor is soft. He looks down and sees it is not wooden, but grass, as if the house has been lifted and planted on top of a field somewhere.

There are four holes in the ground and next to each one is a mound of earth. He hesitates and then approaches them. There is a coffin at the bottom of each hole with an inscription on each one: Mum, then Dad. The third and fourth boxes are empty.

Outside the dogs are barking and clawing at the door, desperate to get inside and finish him off. The door is weak and flies open. He spins round but the dogs are upon him, tearing the flesh from his bones. He screams.

Will wakes trembling, with tears streaming down his face and a savage pain in his head that feels like an ice pick is lodged in his brain. Shivering, he rubs the back of his head; his hair is stiff, matted with dried blood and there is a dull ache in his chest, which makes it hard to breath. He is naked and wrapped in a rough blanket that scratches his skin. His mind whirls in confusion. He recalls being in the cold sea, swimming for his life. It had not been a dream. But how did he get here?

He pushes himself up, but his head spins and his chest feels like it has been hit by a train. He breathes slowly and lets his eyes focus. He is in a dimly lit room that feels like it is moving, creaking, shifting up, then down. He hears the lapping sound of water. There is a round window through which he can see the night sky. He is in the cabin of a boat. He looks to his right. Hanging nearby, over a small oven, is a blazer, a white shirt, trousers, socks, underwear and, on the floor, a soggy pair of brown brogues.

'You're lucky to be alive,' comes a voice.

Will jolts and looks in its direction. Sitting at a small table in a corner is an older gentleman. His hair is white and his face weathered and striking. He is smoking a pipe; the air is fragrant with its sweet, pungent tobacco.

'Who are you?'

'You can call me Skipper. Everyone does.'

'Where am I?'

'You're on board *The Outcast*.'

'*The Outcast*?'

'Part-time tugger; part-time fishin' service. Got me quite a catch tonight, I'd say.'

Will rubs his head. 'I… I was in the sea. But how?'

The old man puffs on his pipe and considers his reply. After a moment, he speaks. 'Someone put you there.'

Will frowns, which makes his head hurt more.

'I don't understand…'

'Neither do I,' says the old man, blowing out a ring of smoke. 'By the looks of it you associate with some dangerous folk.'

Will does not know what the old man is talking about. His memory is foggy, his head dizzy.

The old man continues, 'Tell me, lad. Did they have an accent, a German one perhaps?'

The pain in his head intensifies, like a hammer on his brain. In his mind he can hear voices, like whispers in the wind. But they mean nothing to him.

'Why is that important?'

Skipper's eyes widen and his brow wrinkles.

'You took quite a knock on the head, it'd seem. You do know there's a war on?'

Will stiffens. 'A war?'

'The Germans are bombin' us and we are bombin' them. Nasty business.'

Will closes his eyes in an effort to get to grips with this strange piece of news, but the pain in his head distracts him. He gently places his hand over his temple to ease it, but it does not feel better.

The old man glances at the table and picks up a parcel, the size of a book. 'I'd say this saved your life.'

Will stares hard at it. It seems familiar but he does not know why. There is a hole in the centre with something lodged inside. He feels suddenly cold. It's a bullet.

Skipper pulls a box of matches from his pocket, lights one and places the small fire in the pipe. 'It was the queerest thing. Never saw anything like it. I saw them chase you. I saw them fall to the ground and then I saw one of them shoot you.'

Will pales and rubs the stiff muscles of his chest.

'Why were they trying to kill you?'

Swallowing, he shakes his head and pulls the blanket over his shoulders. He has no idea what the old man is talking about.

The old man is watching him carefully, assessing him.

'I don't know what business any group of men has shooting someone like that. Don't make no sense. How old are you, lad?'

Will furrows his brow as he tries to remember. He isn't entirely sure. The man is calling him 'lad'. He knows he is young. Is he eighteen? Twenty? He could be twenty-five or older for all he knows. 'I... I'm not sure.'

'Do you remember your name?'

'I... I really don't know. I only know I was in the water.'

'Do you remember anything at all?'

He tries hard to recall but the whispering voices have gone and there is nothing for him to latch on to. He shakes his head.

'A friend o' mine took a knock to the head once. Couldn't remember who he was. Didn't recognise his wife nor kids nor pals for that matter. He couldn't do his job neither. He knew his town and where he lived alright. He remembered places, but not people. It were like a whole layer of his memory had gone forever. It were funny at first, but eventually it drove him mad. He had to be "put away" in the end.'

'Did he get his memory back?'

Skipper shakes his head. 'He died alone, as a stranger, even to himself. Sad really.'

Shivering, Will pulls the blanket over his shoulders.

Skipper regards him thoughtfully, 'Whoever those men were, they might well be lookin' for you at Hastings. I reckon it's not safe to go back there. Tonight, I will do a spot o' fishin'. Not supposed to, mind, in these times n' all, but people got to eat and I has to make ends meet. I'll be takin' my haul to London town tomorrow morning. You can talk to the police and maybe see a doctor about that head of yours.'

Will manages a half smile and rests his head back. His eyes feel heavy, and despite his predicament and poor physical state, he soon falls asleep.

Chapter 5

The Parcel is Opened

Sunday, 4th May 1941

Will sleeps fitfully and wakes the following morning to the sound of the boat's chugging engine.

Bright morning light from the porthole dazzles him. His head throbs as his eyes adjust and take in the cabin. It looks different in daylight: even shabbier than his first impression yet it has an order and calmness that gives him a measure of comfort. He sees the table in the corner where Skipper sat last night; on top is a washbowl, a small mirror and a small, neatly folded towel. They weren't there last night. His rescuer must have left them for him. Behind the table, built into the wall, are shelves containing a neat row of books and general bits – fishing tools, a telescope, a conch and a collection of pipes. The only things that seem out of place are his clothes, hanging to dry, and the strange parcel, resting on top of the stove. The parcel with the bullet lodged inside – the bullet meant for him. He swallows hard.

What happened last night?

He has no idea. Strangely he is not frightened, instead he feels a peculiar emptiness as if he is detached from the world and not inhabiting his own body but looking down from above.

He gets up and shivers. The air is crisp and cold, the fire in the small oven having long gone out.

His mind is full of questions. Who is he? Who would want to kill him and why? But he does not have the answers. It seems his memories, and his hope of understanding who he is and why someone tried to kill him, are lost at sea. Wrapped in the blanket, he shuffles to where the clothes hang. Mercifully they are dry. He puts them on, ties up his brogues, ignoring the pain in his head and chest. The clothes are snug and seem expensive, like they belong to a private school.

Are my parents wealthy?

He checks the blazer for an emblem but there is nothing inside or out. Like him, it has no identity. There is a hole where the bullet penetrated. He's surprised at how little it troubles him. There is something hard in the bottom of his right sleeve. Peering inside, he sees what looks like a row of tools neatly secreted into the lining above the wrist. One by one, he takes them out and examines them. One is a narrow pipe, another a small pair of scissors that look like they are made for cutting something stronger than paper or hair – wire cutters! Why would he have these? There is also a pencil-sized piece of steel with a slight curve at one end. At first he thinks it some sort of surgeon's utensil, but that doesn't seem right. He realises it is a lock pick. How he knows this, he cannot say. He does not know what to make of these items and clumsily bundles them back into their hiding places before Skipper appears.

Confused, he distracts himself by washing his face in the bowl of water. Peering through the mirror, he scrubs the dried blood from his hair and assesses his reflection in the mottled glass. His face looks young. His wet hair is inky black, his eyes dark, with a hint of sadness and a look of cold determination. He does not recognise the person looking back at him. It is like gazing at a stranger.

'Who are you? What happened to you?' he says, frowning. He is overcome with a desire to know. Perhaps there is a clue in the parcel – a phone number or an address that will explain his identity and why he was nearly killed last night.

It is wrapped in damp green oilskin with some sort of Greek cross woven into the fabric. In the centre of the cross, the bullet is lodged. He runs his fingers over the small cold projectile that should, by all accounts, be lodged in his dead heart. Trembling, he rubs his chest and feels anger at whoever it was tried to kill him, rather than fear.

What about my mum and dad? They must be worried sick.

He tries to unwrap the parcel, but it is stitched together and sealed with some sort of wax. He uses the wire cutters to break the wax seal and open the threads.

There is a tatty black leather bound notebook inside. He takes it out and leafs carefully through the pages, which are dry and delicate. The notebook is old. There is a lot of handwritten text in a language he does not recognise. There are strange symbols including stars, half-moons, scythes, swastikas and upturned crosses. There are etchings and fine drawings of people from long ago including a sketch of a woman from ancient times, possibly Roman or Greek. She is standing over a stone table containing what looks like a cluster of glowing rocks. There is a second sketch of a jewelled crucifix with very short arms. There is much more but none of it makes any sense. Something falls from the pages onto the table. It is a small card inscribed:

Timothy Chittlock
Room 7
64 Baker Street
London

Timothy Chittlock?

Is that my name? Or if not mine, could it be my father? Do I live on Baker Street?

He tries to remember, but nothing seems familiar. But this is surely a good sign. A clue to who he is? He leaves the cabin to get some air and tell Skipper what he has found. Perhaps the old man can offer him some wisdom.

Outside, on the deck, the morning air is fresh, crisp and salty. There are a dozen modest crates of iced fish at the rear of the small boat. The sea is calmer than it was the night before and in the distance, he can see land. Skipper is smoking his pipe in the steering room at the front of the boat.

'Morning, Skipper.'

'Morning, lad. You seem a lot jollier.' He smiles. 'Glad to see you in such good spirits.'

'I opened the parcel. It contains a notebook, and this card, with the name Timothy Chittlock of 64 Baker Street, London. That could be me, or perhaps my father.'

'That's a fine clue, I'd reckon,' laughs Skipper. 'Don't mean much to me, but I'm sure your neighbour, a certain Mr Sherlock Holmes, could work it out in a blink of an eye.'

Will smiles. 'You do know Sherlock Holmes is a fictional character?'

Skipper laughs so hard he coughs, doubling over to spit into a spittoon. He pats Will on the back and then looks through his binoculars across the water. His brow furrows.

'What is it, Skipper?' But then he hears it. The chugging sound of another boat.

'Get inside, and stay out of sight.'

Will hurries into the steering room and crouches down. Instinctively he scans the interior searching for something hard: a crowbar, an ice pick, anything to defend himself. A coldness sweeps over him. But that isn't all: he does not feel frightened, he is excited and confident. His breathing increases rapidly.

Who am I?

Outside, he can hear the other boat approaching. Minutes later, the chugging of *The Outcast* and the other boat stops.

'Mornin', Skip,' says a voice from the other boat.

'Ned,' says Skipper, in a gruff response.

'Quite a haul you got there.'

'Yup.'

'Takin' to market, are ya?'

'Where else would I take it?'

'No need to be like that, Skip. Especially, as I have some news concernin' you and that rust bucket.'

'Oh yes,' replies an unconvinced Skipper. 'And just what would that be?'

'There are some men waitin' at the docks. They say they are police, but they don't look like police to me. Asking around about a boat called *The Outcast,* they are. A boat what was seen leaving Hastings last night. Appears they are looking for some cargo it might be carrying. "But he only carries fish," I tells them.'

In the steering room Will stiffens and holds his breath. He peeks out at Skipper who appears calm, but his fists are clenched, his knuckles white.

'Did I see someone onboard with you, Skip?'

'I'd say you were mistaken, Ned. Just me and my fish. That's all.'

'Is that right?' says Ned, 'And how about you give me those fish and we'll say nothing more of it.'

Skipper's expression is fixed, he is giving away no secrets.

'I'll give them as a goodwill gesture for you and your family,' says Skipper.

'I knew you'd see reason.'

In the steering room, Will feels guilty and angry at this man for forcing Skipper to give up his fish, just to protect him. He hears Skipper passing the crates across to the other boat.

'That's the lot,' says Skipper.

'You don't 'alf get yourself into some scrapes, old man.'

'You've got what you wanted. Now be off with you.'

The other boat's engine starts up and Will feels an overwhelming sense of relief.

'Watch your back, old man!' calls Ned, like some final grim warning.

Skipper returns to the steering room, his fixed expression transformed into a wide-eyed determined look like a wrinkled boy wanting adventure.

'I'm sorry,' says Will.

Skipper starts up the engine and looks at him thoughtfully, 'He's a treacherous swine, that Ned. Don't be sorry, lad. Besides, I don't like the sound of these men, whoever they may be. We're going to change routes. I'll get you to London safely. I promise.'

'Thank you for helping me.'

'There is a reason I called this boat *The Outcast*. A damn fine reason. And that's why idiots like that Ned don't care much for me.'

Skipper lights his pipe and steers a new course. At last there is a sense of hope.

Chapter 6

Into the Hornet's Nest

It is late afternoon as Skipper steers the boat through the Thames estuary, watching for signs of any suspicious activity or unfamiliar boats. He sees nothing, but nevertheless he proceeds with caution. The closer they get to the docks, the more dangerous it will be for both him and the frightened, disoriented young man he pulled from the sea. For reasons he cannot explain, Skipper feels an affinity with him. Despite his amnesia he can see a strength and determination that might just see him through whatever trouble he is in. He fancies he is like him: an outsider, an outcast. The lad survived the guns of half a dozen men, including a direct hit aimed at his heart. He also survived a drowning. The lad is special and – different. There is a reason he must live. Skipper has no idea what that reason might be, but he feels it and is prepared to risk everything to ensure it. What did it matter anyway? The life of an outcast is a life of risk. He smiles to himself and puffs on his pipe.

Leaving the estuary behind them, they pass Tilbury, then Dagenham. The river narrows as they approach the London docklands. Skipper draws the curtains on the steering cabin's side windows so that the only view in and out is through the front window.

'We're approaching the hornet's nest,' says Skipper. 'Stand behind me, lad, in the shadows, and keep an eye on the bank on either side. Maybe you'll see a face that will jog your memory.' He hands the boy the binoculars. 'Seems there was an air raid last night.'

Will peers through the binoculars and carefully watches the approach. He feels his heart quickening, not from fear, but from excitement, as if he is returning home after a long arduous trip away. There is a familiarity to the skyline that warms his heart and almost confirms that Baker Street must be his home after all. Yet there is something wrong with this version of the city. Skipper had told him more about the war and the nightly bombings the city endured. It was hard to absorb. On either side of the river, commercial offices and warehouses dealing in imports and exports would once have lined these waters. But today they are rubble and ruins decimated by Nazi bombers. Across the city, plumes of smoke rise up into a slate grey sky where giant fishlike barrage balloons are tethered to the ground below. It is like he has stepped into a ravaged and torn city, like something from an H.G. Wells novel. It is so hard to take in. The London he thinks he remembers is not the London he sees before him. He fears for the city and its people. He fears for his family and wonders where they could be.

Has Baker Street survived the bombs?

He trembles inside.

'Just up there, to my left, are two men. They're watching us and they don't look like dockers,' says Skipper.

Through the binoculars, Will sees two men dressed in smart suits and trilbies, watching *The Outcast* approach. Their expressions and body language suggests they are doing more than enjoying a leisurely day out.

There is a car pulling up behind them; it is an Austin 8.

The door opens and another man gets out. He looms over the other two and looks towards *The Outcast*. He is thickset, with dark cropped hair and a bushy black moustache that partially obscures a grim expression.

Knots form in Will's stomach, his breathing quickens.

'Skipper, I know that man. I don't know how, but I know him.'

'He's a dangerous-looking sort, alright.'

The three men get into the car and begin driving alongside the river.

'There's another to the right,' says Skipper.

29

Will turns to the other side of the dock and sees a man dressed in a black suit, black shirt and gloves. Will thinks he might be some sort of priest. He is watching the Austin 8, and occasionally glances at *The Outcast*, as he strolls along. His cheeks are sunken, his eyes are like hollows, his hair is long and white and stretched across the top of his head. For a second Will thinks he sees the glint of blue steel in his hand. But it is gone, perhaps a trick of the light. Nevertheless, his skin crawls for reasons he cannot explain.

'Can we go faster?' he asks.

Skipper smiles, conspiratorially. 'I think we ought to,' he says, and pushes *The Outcast* forward.

Chapter 7

Trouble at Tower Bridge

Ahead Will can see Tower Bridge in all its hulking magnificence. He is relieved to see it is undamaged and still functional. Red double-decker buses, cars and people pass across it and for a second it seems life in London is normal and there is no war.

Skipper interrupts his thoughts. 'Those men can't drive along this side of the dock. Reckon they will take a fast road to the next stop and cut us off. We'll stop at St Katherine's Dock. It's not used any longer. The bombs have decimated it, but it will be a good springboard for us to get to Baker Street.'

'Us?'

'I'll see you through to the end, lad. I made a promise to myself, I did. There are dangerous men following you and I won't let them have another pop at you with their guns.'

'But...'

'No buts, lad. You ain't gettin' a choice.' Skipper smiles warmly.

Will is grateful to the older man, and secretly relieved that he will not be alone for the journey to Baker Street.

'We'll be there shortly, so get ready to hurry.'

Will nods, and feels an odd sense of calm and purpose. He is ready, he is always ready. He steadies his breathing, all the while his eyes scan the riverbanks for unwelcome faces. His palm touches the side pocket of his blazer, where the notebook is safely tucked.

It is now evening. After tying the boat to what remains of the dock, they hurry along St Katherine's Way and up to Tower Bridge Approach, where they dodge people enjoying the weekend break.

From somewhere below the bridge the pounding drums and the melodic trumpet of a brass band fills the air. It sounds like the Salvation Army. A woman starts to sing heartily at the top of her voice.

Down at the cross where my saviour died,
Down where the cleansing of sin I cried,
There to my heart was the blood applied;
Glory to his name

Traffic is slow. The wartime lights-out rule hinders progress. With Skipper behind him, he pushes his way through the crowd. He hears three thumps and halts. The crowd gasps. The bridge trembles and the dark waters of the Thames shiver. The thunder of distant explosions reverberates across the city and in the east the evening sky fills with flashes of bright white light. It is then, better late than never, that a siren wails its warning. Panic ripples through the crowd and they begin running, desperate to get across the bridge and into shelter. Will is herded by the crowd and separated from the old fisherman.

'Skipper!' he shouts, but there is no response.

He forces his way through the crowd on the side of the bridge, clinging on to the steel girders. He swears he hears a gunshot. And then above the din he hears someone shout.

'My lad, wait!'

The crowd thins and Will turns to see Skipper limping toward him. He falls forward, and Will just manages to catch him. He is surprisingly light and feels more a like a sack of bones than a grown man. His chest is wheezing and he is sweating as if he had just run a marathon. He groans, but his voice is rasping, his breath short.

He steadies the old man, who seems a shadow of who he was.

'Skipper, what's happened?' he says, confused and mindful of the approaching bombers. 'We must get off the bridge.'

'Too late for me. You must go. You are in danger, lad … grave danger.'

There's a loud bang and Will feels the old man jerk and stiffen. His face contorts with pain, his eyes flutter and he slumps forward. Confused, Will catches him, supporting his back and feels something warm and sticky on Skipper's jumper. He lowers him to the ground and looks at his hand. There is blood on his fingers.

'Help, someone help,' he calls, but the bridge is empty.

They are alone. The only sound is the approaching drone of bombers and the hymn of the Salvation Army songstress who, it seems, has been abandoned by her band.

The old man's eyes flicker and close.

'Skipper, Skipper!' Will shakes the old seaman in an effort to revive him, but there is no response. And then, from somewhere nearby, a man's voice starts to sing along with the hymn.

Down at the cross where my saviour died,
Down where the cleansing of sin I cried,
There to my heart was the blood applied;
Glory to his name

On the opposite side of the bridge, a man is approaching. He is dressed in a black suit and has long white hair. It is the priest-man he saw on the riverbank.

'Please, help us! This man is hurt.'

The man walks slowly toward them. As he draws closer, the feeling of unease that Will felt at the dock returns. His stomach tingles. Something is not quite right.

The man crouches down beside them, cocks his head to the side and gazes over Skipper. His eyes are like dark hollows and seem devoid of emotion.

Will's instincts tell him to run, but he cannot leave Skipper. Not after he saved his life.

And then the man falls onto his knees, looming over the old fisherman like a cobra. He removes his gloves, 'Pray with me, boy.'

'Please, help me get him off the bridge and to a doctor.'

'Don't you recognise me, boy?' he says, his hands clasping together.

'No. Who are you?'

The priest-man dips his head and mutters something under his breath. Will notices his hands are scarred with dozens of crucifixes carved into his flesh. Some of the scars are bloody and recent. Will jolts as a memory flashes in his mind – an image of this man, his face contorted, his arm raised and, in his hand, a blade. He knows this man – but how? On the tip of his tongue is a name. Will frowns…

The holy man… no… the Pastor. He is known as the Pastor.

But this man of God doesn't make Will feel safe – quite the opposite.

The Pastor finishes the prayer and begins rummaging in Skipper's pockets.

'What are you doing?' Will feels a swelling anger that this stranger should dare to search Skipper's pockets. He grabs the man's forearm. 'Leave him alone.'

The Pastor smiles, his teeth are small, like a child's.

The hairs on Will's neck bristle, 'Maybe we should get the police.'

'There is no need for the law,' the Pastor says, glancing at the bullet hole on Will's blazer. 'You look like you have been in a spot of bother yourself.'

Will swallows and does not reply.

The Pastor gets to his feet. His jacket falls open. There is something dark and metal tucked into his belt. A pistol! What kind of holy-man carries a pistol?

'Do you have it?' he asks.

The crump, crump, crump of falling bombs is getting closer.

'I don't know what you are talking about.'

Something slips from the Pastor's sleeve and into his hand. It is a long and shiny razor.

34

'Do not lie to me, young man.'

And then, Skipper springs to life and grabs the man's hand. He bites into his flesh and the blade falls to the ground.

'Run, lad, run!' he shouts.

Pulse racing, Will edges back, torn between running and staying to help his friend. But the Pastor is nimble. He pulls out the gun with his free hand and shoots the old man.

Will stumbles backward, watching Skipper jerk twice as two more bullets are pumped into his frail body.

The Pastor looks up, his previously emotionless eyes betraying a simmering rage.

With his heart rattling in his chest, Will backs quickly away, picks up his pace and runs, hiding wherever he can behind the cover of abandoned buses and cars.

Chapter 8

The Pastor strikes

Wailing sirens, droning bombers and falling whistlers fade to background noise as Will sprints through the dark, empty streets, panting. His brow is clammy, his heart is pounding, but it is also heavy. He tries to make sense of what has just happened. He is to blame. If it weren't for him, Skipper would be alive and well and steering his boat happily up the Thames. Every muscle in Will's body seems to twist as he thinks of Skipper's cold-blooded murder. He ducks into an alleyway and retreats into the shadows to catch his breath and think. His head throbs, a dull pulsing ache that does not want to go away.

Despite all the noise, he can just make out the clip of footsteps approaching and snatches of that same hymn. He feels his skin crawling and hurries out of the alleyway and on into a street of Victorian terraces. He looks around for somewhere to hide, an empty house perhaps. A sudden flash in the sky lights up the street and he feels horribly exposed and alone. There is no one else around, no one to call to for help. Everyone will be taking shelter in their cellars or the Underground. He hurries along the street and crosses into another darkened alleyway.

He stops at a rusty gate, the entrance to a rear garden, and looks back up the alleyway. The Pastor is there, stopped at the far end, peering in his direction. Will backs into the shadows, holding his breath and praying for him to move on. To his relief, he does.

He peers beyond the gate. The garden is overgrown and full of rag-and-bone booty probably looted from bomb-damaged homes. There is a three-wheeled pram, stacks of wooden crates and various forgotten toys, including dolls with missing eyes and limbs. He wonders if the house has been abandoned. It has the look of neglect about it. Pushing the gate open, he hurries toward the rear door, but it is locked. He remembers the lock pick in his sleeve and goes to work, wondering where and how he has learned to pick locks.

Am I some sort of criminal, or thief?

Footsteps crunch in the alleyway and he leans toward the lock. With a surgeon's lightness of touch, he feels for the pressure points, pushes them, and hears the clicking sound of the lock opening.

Slipping quietly inside, he closes the door behind him. In the darkness, he stumbles forward and knocks over a kitchen chair. He swears under his breath at the noise. He leaves the kitchen and slides up the hallway. He freezes, thinking he hears someone at the front door. And then the back door opens. Framed inside, like an image from a nightmare, is the Pastor.

He springs forward, rushing at Will, with one hand reaching for his throat.

Will does not retreat. Something in him, an instinct, makes him stand still, his eyes taking in the Pastor's every move. At the right moment, he grabs the man's wrist and kicks him savagely between the legs. The Pastor grunts, but clings to him like a parasite. They fall backwards through a door and into the living room.

The Pastor is fast and reacts quickly, pinning Will up against the wall by his neck. Their faces are inches apart, the air between them sour with what smells like rotten meat. The man's grip is tight, Will gasps for air and tries to push him away, but the older man is too strong.

The house shakes as a bomb explodes nearby. Dust falls from the ceiling, coating Will's shoulders and clammy face.

The Pastor's small eyes flash, 'And there fell upon men a great hail out of heaven, and men blasphemed God because of the plague of the hail; for the plague thereof was exceeding great…'

He slams his fist into Will's stomach and releases his grip.

Whatever air was left in Will's lungs shoots out and he crumples to the floor in pain, clutching his stomach. More bombs fall, shaking the foundations. The dusty wooden floorboards vibrate against his cheek.

'…And men were scorched with great heat, and blasphemed the name of God…'

The Pastor crouches beside him, searches his pockets and takes out the notebook.

'Well, well,' he says, leafing through it tentatively. His eyes widen, his neck turns red, 'It pains me to think you would hide this from me.'

Pushing himself up, Will does not know what to say. What is so important about this notebook?

Will is hauled to his feet by his hair, 'Who are you, boy?'

'No one…' but then he hears a whine coming from the kitchen. It is followed by a snarl and a growl and then a gravelly voice says, 'What the hell?'

The Pastor places a razor against Will's throat, 'Do not say a word, boy.'

The dog barks and claws scrape on wood.

The gravel-voiced man shouts, 'Spitfire, NO!'

But the dog skids into the room. It is a squat white bull terrier with a scarred face, its eyes locked firmly on Will. It springs forward, teeth bared in a vicious smile. The Pastor is distracted for a split second. Will grabs his forearm and holds it. The dog's jaws lock onto the arm and clamp shut. The Pastor cries out and tries to shake the dog off, but Spitfire bites harder. The Pastor falls back, dropping the razor and notebook on the floor.

This is Will's moment to act. He should run; but not without the notebook. It is his and he wants answers. He leaps forward and grabs it.

The Pastor swipes out at him and misses by an inch.

Will can see his free hand searching the floor for the blade. He turns to run but a broad man is standing in the doorway with a strip of lead pipe in his hand.

'Mister, we have to get out of here.'

There is a horrific yelp followed by a feeble whimper. He turns to see the Pastor pushing Spitfire's limp body onto the floor. In his hand is the razor, wet with blood.

'Spitfire! Spitfire, my boy.' The animal's breathing is shallow. Will is no expert but he could guess he was a goner.

The Pastor leaps to his feet, his expression demonic. The large man looks from his dog to the Pastor, his face burning with rage. He lifts the strip of lead and lunges at the holy man.

With the notebook tucked into his blazer, Will runs up the hall and out the front door, his head reeling.

Outside, he bumps into a small boy who is hurrying past, carrying a crate of food. The small boy glances at the house Will has just emerged from then back at Will. He jumps as two gunshots are fired inside.

'Follow me,' says the boy.

Will sees some other boys and a girl, exiting various houses on the same street. They are all carrying similar small crates of food. Will knows he must run, but he does not know where. His memory is shattered, he does not know who he is or what he is. He needs time to think. Perhaps the boy can give him shelter until he gathers his thoughts. Glancing back, he sees the Pastor emerge from the house, limping badly. He is in no position to follow them. Will almost wants to cheer, but he follows the boy and disappears into the shadows of the street.

Chapter 9

Sam

Will follows the boy along Fenchurch Street and up a back street. The others are running in single file behind the girl, who seems to be in charge. There are seven in total, eight including the girl. They stop by a pair of tall wooden doors, which look like the entrance to some sort of yard. The girl glances up and down the street before entering through a small hatch in one of the doors. The others follow her through. Will holds back, closes his eyes and rubs his throbbing head. He thinks about his fight and wonders how he learned to defend himself so well. And then there is the tailored blazer with its secreted tools. Just who is he?

A voice disturbs his thoughts. 'Are you alright? You don't look well.'

It is the small boy; he is smiling. He looks around twelve years old and has short cropped blond hair, a dirty face and a snub nose. 'I'm Sam.' he says.

He has no name to give in return. There is nothing in the folds of his memory, a first name, a surname or even a letter, as a clue to his identity. There is just the name from the notebook.

'Tim… My name is Tim.'

'Nice to meet you, Tim. Come inside. You'll be safer.'

Tim is not his name. He does not know how he knows this. He just does. He looks back to check he hasn't been followed. The street is clear, so he lets Sam lead him through the hatch.

The yard looks like an unused tradesman's work area. Dominating the space is a red double-decker bus with union flags hanging from its upstairs windows and an elaborately framed portrait of the royal family fixed to the side panel. The rear platform is draped in a plush red velvet curtain of the sort you might find in an theatre. The whole set up looks like some sort of patriotic, mobile den.

To the left of the bus is a makeshift table made from several heavy planks of wood resting on stacked-up bus tyres. The other children have put their crates on top and are standing around it. They are looking at him suspiciously and seem oblivious to the world beyond the yard where the skies flash and the bombs are still falling.

'Who the 'ell are you?' asks the girl, her brow furrowed. She seems to be the oldest, fourteen Will reckons, a wiry strong frame with mousey brown hair cut just below the ears. She marches forward and stands inches from him, her arms folded, her eyes wary.

'He's with me, Kitty,' says Sam, sheepishly.

Kitty looks at Sam with an accusing expression. 'Sam Rudge, what have I told you about bringing strangers home. We ain't got the food. Besides, he looks old enough to look after himself!'

Kitty has an air of authority, a maternal protective edge to her that Will can't help but admire.

'But he was in trouble, Kitty. You're always saying we gotta 'elp people. Not just ourselves. So I just 'elped him.'

The other boys circle around warily watching Will who is bigger and older than them. Suddenly they don't seem like children anymore. One is holding an old tennis racquet, someone else brandishes a cracked cricket bat, another holds a length of chain and one particularly angry-looking boy with puffy eyes and large freckles sidles up with a grubby machete and pokes Will in the chest with it.

Despite his chest muscles being tender, Will surprises himself by not flinching. He scans the approaching boys and calculates the order in which he will disarm each one. The machete boy will be first. He has no discernible

41

skill with the weapon he is holding. Will will grab his wrist, break it in one hit, and relieve him of the machete. He feels his heart beat faster. But he holds back, frightened at what he is capable of.

Who am I?

'What sort of trouble are you in?' says Kitty, interrupting his thoughts.

'He was robbin' Bob Batten's house,' says Sam.

There is a collective gasp from everyone in the yard.

'You've got some nerve, robbin' Bob Batten's gaff,' says Kitty. 'He'll flay you alive if he finds you.'

Sam continues, 'I heard gunshots coming from his house. Not one but two!'

The others start murmuring amongst themselves.

Kitty's eyes widen, she leans forward. 'Is Bob Batten dead? Did you kill him?'

'No. Nor did I rob him.'

Kitty squares up to him, her nose almost touching his chin. 'Then what are you doing in our patch?'

He hesitates before answering. He does not see the value in lying. Besides, he could use some friends and perhaps if he tells the truth they might help him.

'I was hiding in that house. A man is trying to kill me.'

'He's lying!' says the machete boy.

'No 'e's not. I 'eard the gunshots, remember?' says Sam.

'Who's trying to kill you?' demands Kitty.

'I don't know.'

'Why's he want you dead, then?'

'I don't know and I intend to find out.'

Kitty eyes him suspiciously, but he keeps his expression fixed and calm. After a moment she seems to relax.

'Alright. You can stay here for a bit, but don't you try anything. We'll be watching.'

'I will leave in the morning. I promise.'

Kitty nods, curtly. 'Sam, stay with him at all times, you hear?'

'Yes, Kitty,' says a beaming Sam. He turns and grins. 'You hungry, Tim?'

Will pats his stomach and remembers he hasn't eaten in quite a while, 'Maybe a little.'

Sam runs to the table and grabs two apples and a small block of cheese. 'Follow me,' he says, hurrying to the bus and through the red curtain.

Will follows him. The downstairs of the bus has no passenger seats. In their place are sofas, cushions and rugs, plundered presumably from other people's houses. There is a musty odour, a lingering smell of unwashed boys.

'Up 'ere,' calls Sam.

Will makes his way up the stairs and is unsurprised to see the top deck kitted out with bunks, mostly unmade. Sam is sitting at the front eating the apple and cheese.

'Come and eat, Tim.'

Will sits beside him. 'Where are your parents, Sam?'

'Dead. All our parents are dead. Some of us are the forgotten kids who didn't get evacuated. Others, like Kitty, refused to leave London. This is 'er dad's place. He was a mechanic before 'e was killed in the war. 'Er mother died when their house was bombed. Kitty was out looking for food. She found us and took us all in.'

'But why steal food from people?'

'We don't steal everything. We just take some of it and sometimes we give some away, if it's some old dear who's 'ard up. It's what we do. We're like Robin Hood's Merry Men.'

Will smiles and bites into the apple, which is juicy and delicious.

'Eat some cheese at the same time? It is so good!'

Will takes a bite from the cheese and eats it alongside the apple. Sam is right. It is delicious. He smiles at Sam and garbles his approval, spitting apple as he does.

Sam finds this hugely funny and can't stop laughing. Will laughs too and for a second forgets the horrible nightmare he has woken up to.

'What next?' says Sam. 'Are you going to find that man?'

'No. I need to get home and find my parents. They live in Baker Street, I think. Then I can go to the police.'

Sam nods, 'I'll 'elp you.'

'No!' Will replies too sharply. Sam looks hurt. 'I'm sorry, Sam. It's dangerous out there. I don't know if Bob Batten is dead. My guess is, he is. And he's not the first. Someone else was killed today. Someone who saved my life and wanted to help me.'

'Who?'

'It doesn't matter. It's just too dangerous. First thing tomorrow, I will go home. You stay here. It'll be safer.'

Sam says nothing for a moment and then smiles. 'You're right, Tim. It's safer here.'

Chapter 10

64 Baker Street

Monday, 5th May 1941

The air raid is over and dawn is breaking. Will spent the night lying with Sam on his bunk, but has barely slept. The events of the past twenty-four hours have played on his mind and he is impatient to get to Baker Street. He rises slowly, trying his best not to wake his new young friend. The others are quietly snoring and don't stir as he slips nimbly across the deck and down the stairs, carrying his shoes.

Outside, the skies are clear of bombers but thick with dust and the stench of smoke and cordite.

He is unsure where he is and heads back toward Fenchurch Street. He knows he must head west. Hurrying on, he sees people, wrapped in coats and blankets, trickling from the shelter of Underground stations. Their faces are grey and grim and he suspects they are clinging on to the hope that their homes have survived the attack.

He has the sensation he is being watched and followed. He does not look behind him but carries on, quickly but trying to seem casual, fearing that the Pastor has caught up with him. Turning a corner, he lurks in the dark recess of a doorway, his stomach clenched, his fists curled in preparation for a fight.

Moments pass before a small boy with blond hair and a dirty face appears.

'Sam!'

Sam almost jumps out of skin and clutches his chest, 'Stone the crows, Tim. You didn't 'alf give me a fright.'

'What are you doing here?'

'You need help and I am 'ere to help you.'

'Go home, Sam.'

'Can't do that, Tim. Kitty says I have to keep an eye on you.'

'Baker Street is not your patch.'

'All o' London is our patch, Tim. All of it.'

Will glances up and down the street. There does not seem to be anyone suspicious watching them. No sign of the Pastor, or those other men in the Austin 8. If anyone was watching, they would have clocked Sam by now and it would already be too late. Perhaps they had already seen him when they were running from Bob Batten's house last night. Maybe Sam will be safer if he keeps him close, for now. Will frowns at Sam and pulls him back into the doorway. 'You stick close to me and don't do anything unless I tell you.'

Sam salutes and smiles, 'Yes, sir! Lead on.'

Will tries to figure the quickest route.

As if reading his thoughts Sam says, 'I know the way.'

Will squeezes Sam's shoulder, 'Lead on,' he says with a smile.

Sam beams back but Will feels a sudden sense of dread – two men have died already. Will does not want Sam becoming another victim. If he has to, he will kill to prevent that happening. But for now he needs Sam. Once they get to Baker Street he will do whatever it takes to get him safely home.

They arrive at Baker Street around ninety minutes later. Number 64 is a vast stone-fronted office block and not a home, as he was expecting. Perhaps his father works here.

The entrance has double doors with a lock that is too big for his pick. The front windows are strong, thick and impenetrable. The place is like a fortress. There is no way in from the front.

'What is this place?' asks Sam.

'I don't know.'

Will wonders about other access points and walks further along Baker Street. At the next left, he finds a narrow lane leading to the rear of the building. There is a tradesman's entrance with a lock that is small and easy to pick. Not such a fortress after all.

The door opens into a kitchen area with rows of teapots, stacks of plates, pots and pans. With Sam in tow, he makes his way down a hallway and follows it through to the front double doors. He notices a room list on the wall. Room 7 is on the lower ground floor. They make their way down and find room 7 at the end of the corridor. They stop outside and Will places his ear to the door. Sam does the same. Satisfied there is no one inside, Will turns the doorknob and pushes the door open.

The room smells of lavender wood polish. The curtains are drawn. Will fumbles for the light switch, turns it on and sees a desk with a telephone. Behind it is a bank of filing cabinets and, pinned to the walls, are maps of the United Kingdom, Ireland, France, Germany, Russia and Poland.

'It's an office of some sort,' says Sam, stating the obvious. 'Looking at those maps, I'd reckon there is a connection to the war.'

Will had thought the same. What he knows about the war is what Skipper told him on the way to London. It was all so unbelievable. He feels strangely inadequate and is suddenly glad he has Sam to help fill in the blanks. He thinks he might tell Sam everything about his memory loss later.

He glances at the filing cabinets, which are labelled alphabetically. He opens one of them. There are rows of files listed by surnames, none of which he recognises.

Under C, he finds a file labelled *Chittlock, Timothy*. He takes it out and opens it. Inside is a photograph of a bespectacled man dressed in a tweed suit, standing in front of a blackboard. His face seems familiar. Will's mind begins to swim and he hears a voice as if it is speaking through a faulty transistor radio. The man talks in reassuring tones, but there is something else. He strains to listen:

'You understand what I am asking you to do?'

His stomach twists. The words don't mean anything to him. But somehow, he knows they must.

'You alright, Tim? You look pale.'

Will shakes his head. 'I… I'm fine, thanks.'

He turns the photograph over. There is writing on the back:

Tim Chittlock, Beaulieu House, Brockenhurst, Hampshire.

'Who is he?' says Sam.

'I thought he was my father, but now I don't think he is.'

'What do you mean, you thought he was your father?'

Will sits at the desk and places his head in his hands. 'Something happened to me, Sam. I lost my memory and all I know is there are men trying to kill me. They have killed two innocent men already and I don't know why.'

'Blimey. You are in a fix.'

'My name is not Tim, either.'

'Ooh. What is it then?'

'I don't know,' Will says and then his attention is drawn to the desktop where a manila folder labelled CLASSIFIED rests. The folder is entitled 'Agents of VIPER'. He feels an odd twinge of familiarity and pulls the folder towards him.

He opens it. There is a photograph on top, a mug shot of a broad-faced man with a stern expression and a thick black moustache. His shoulders stiffen and his fists curl. He is one of the men from the Austin 8 at the riverside yesterday. But there is something else. He is sure he knows this man, knows him so well that he can almost smell his stale body odour. He turns the picture over. Scrawled on the back is a name:

Colonel Victor Frost

Leader, Agents of VIPER.

The man's name rolls through the mists of his mind. He knows it. He knows him. He knows VIPER. But what is VIPER? He scrolls through the other pictures and stops at one, his heart in his mouth.

'Blimey!' says Sam, 'Is that you?'

Will's mouth dries. It is him, a younger version of him. He is perhaps twelve years old, his hair is shorn and he is wearing military fatigues. He turns the photograph over.

Will Starling

Agent of VIPER

That's his name. He's sure of it. Part of him is relieved to know it, but another part of him is horrified to find out he might be in league with these men. It can't be true. They are trying to kill him!

What have I done to make these men want to kill me?

'Will. Your name is Will. Are you some sort of secret agent?' asks Sam, excitedly.

Will does not respond. His heart begins to beat faster.

What does any of this mean? How can I be an agent of this VIPER? And what about my parents?

Somehow, although he cannot remember his family, he can still feel their warmth and love like it is imprinted on his soul.

And why does he have this notebook that so many people want? Why is he wearing a blazer with tools secreted in the lining? The desire to know the truth burns hard inside him. He has another journey to make to track down this Timothy Chittlock. He must go to Beaulieu and find him.

He removes his picture from the file and stuffs it into his pocket. He will burn it later, removing any trace of himself from the VIPER file.

A sudden noise from the corridor makes them both jump. Will places the folder back where it was and switches off the light. Then he hurries toward the windows and opens one. Sam leaps out first followed by Will, who gently closes the window before sprinting away after Sam.

Chapter 11

Wanted

Will looks behind him as he hits the ground and sees the window latch move. He jumps out of view, behind a row of dustbins, pulling Sam with him. They both crouch out of sight. Moments later, heavy footsteps sprint past. Will shudders and wonders which of his enemies it was. Had one of them caught up with him?

He waits five minutes before risking a look beyond the dustbins and up and down the back street. There is no one there.

'Who was that?' says Sam.

'I don't know and I don't think I want to know. Let's go.'

He hurries them away from Baker Street until they reach Park Lane, which is busy with morning traffic and workers beginning their day. He stops and faces Sam.

'Listen up, Sam…'

Sam is beaming, 'This is so exciting!'

Will feels a surge of irritation, 'No, it's not. Two innocent men have been murdered and someone is trying to kill me. It is not exciting, it is terrifying!'

'I'm sorry, I meant…'

Will sighs and places his hand on the boy's shoulder, 'I know what you meant, Sam, and I didn't mean to raise my voice. I don't want anyone else to get hurt. Least of all you. Please, just go back home, stay with Kitty and the others and keep out of sight. You are already in too deep.'

'But I can help you.'

Will feels so desperately isolated, a lump builds in his throat. More than anything, he wants to say yes. He so needs a friend right now, someone he can trust who can see him through this mess. But he cannot risk Sam's life. There is no question of that.

'No, Sam.'

Sam looks to the ground, deflated and hurt.

'When this is over, I will come back and find you. I promise. We can be mates.'

Sam smiles, his face lighting up despite its grubby streaks. 'I'd like that.'

'Me too. Goodbye Sam.'

Sam thrusts his hands in his pockets, and turns to leave. 'Bye, Will.'

With a heavy heart, Will watches him leave, but he knows it is the right decision. When he is satisfied Sam has gone, he gets his bearings for Victoria Station. He spots a figure dip quickly out of view at a nearby shop entrance. For a second he thinks it might have been a shadow. But he cannot take that risk. He swallows and retreats, turning on his heels and running as fast as he can.

He arrives at Victoria where the crowds are flocking to and from the station. He glances across the concourse at the station clock. It is almost 8.20 am. A man is loading the morning papers onto the stand. The headlines are mostly about last night's air raid but one catches his attention.

Two murders during last night's air raid.

His mouth dries. He reads beneath the headline.

Hastings fisherman, Skipper Jones and local man Robert Batten were murdered in cold blood last night. A policeman spokesman said that the murders are believed to be connected and, after an anonymous tip-off, they are searching for a young man believed to be around sixteen years old, name unknown. He is a stocky lad, around 5ft 10 inches, with dark hair and is considered very dangerous. Please contact Scotland Yard with any information.

Will's heart pounds. There is a picture next to the article. It is a rough sketch of him, except he looks angry and dangerous. The Pastor must have lied to the police and given them his description. He edges slowly away from the newsstand. He looks to the platforms. He must get out of London fast.

With his collar up and head down he hurries across to the rail map and traces the line to Hampshire and Beaulieu. Brockenhurst is his destination. He checks the timetable and station clock. The train is leaving in three minutes. He has no money for a ticket and has to think of something fast.

The train is boarding. He searches for a gap in the crowd and edges his way through the melee, allowing himself to be carried along in the mass of people.

The guard blows the whistle and Will hurries through the first open door he sees. He slams it shut and a moment later the train is moving. He threads his way through the busy carriages and finds a compartment taken up by a woman and her three young children: one a small boy who is sucking his thumb and two identical babies who sit crying on her lap. She seems flustered and distracted. Her cases are blocking the aisle.

'Shall I put these away?' says Will politely, hoping she has not seen the morning papers.

The woman looks at him, her gaze lingering suspiciously over the bullet hole in his blazer.

'Just an accident. Mum's going to kill me when she finds out,' he says, smiling sweetly.

The woman sighs, 'Yes, please.'

He lifts the cases onto the rack and out of the corner of his eye sees a figure, inches away, watching him from the corridor. He turns to see a tall, broad man with a neatly trimmed greying beard and short brown hair combed in a side parting. He has green eyes and a serious expression, 'Any seat in here, son?' he says. He has an accent, Irish, perhaps Ulster.

Will realises he is blocking his access into the compartment. The man looks at Will for longer than is comfortable. Will notices he is carrying the newspaper with his picture under his arm. 'No,' he says, sharply.

The man narrows his eyes, then turns away and continues along the corridor in search of another compartment.

Will watches him walk away and is relieved he does not look back. But still, there was something about him that has put him on edge.

He closes the door to the compartment, turns to the woman and gestures at the empty seats. 'May I?'

She nods agreement and he sits down.

'Have you been in a fight?' says the small boy.

'Jimmy Jones!' says his mother, 'don't be rude.'

Will smiles nervously, 'Why do you say that?'

'Your jacket is ripped and dirty.'

'That's enough, Jimmy,' says his mother.

Will looks down at his blazer. The boy is right. There is dust all over him and a rip on his sleeve. What did he expect having been shot, falling into the sea, fighting, and then crawling through windows and hiding behind dustbins. He glances at the woman who is tending her babies. She seems not to have noticed.

'I fought a monster,' says Will, covering the hole in his chest.

The boy stares at him wide-eyed. 'What happened?'

'Jimmy!' cries the woman.

Young Jimmy folds his arms and screws up his face and Will smiles.

The rhythm of the train is soothing and he wants to sleep, but his mind is too busy. He takes the notebook from his pocket and begins leafing through the pages. He finds a sketch of what seems to be a disc with the planets and constellations inside it. Around its perimeter are more of the strange symbols: eyes, pyramids, scythes, swastikas, daggers and upturned crosses.

Thirty minutes pass and he is none the wiser. He glances up and sees the Irishman standing in the corridor and looking into the compartment. Will furtively slips the notebook into his pocket.

'I need to pee,' says Jimmy. His mother ignores him as she wrestles with feeding both babies at the same time. 'Mummy, I need to pee!'

'Just wait, Jimmy!'

Will hears the door of the next compartment slide open. 'Tickets please,' says the guard.

'I can't wait!' says Jimmy.

'I can take him,' Will says.

'Oh, you are a dear, thank you.'

'Come on, Jimmy.' Will extends his hand. 'Let's go and find the lav.'

The boy beams and Will leads him out into the corridor. He ignores the Irishman whose gaze makes him uneasy. He hopes it is his imagination.

'Tickets please,' says the guard, emerging from the next compartment and turning his attention towards Will.

Will gestures at Jimmy's mum, 'Our mum has the tickets, sir. I'm just taking little Jimmy to the toilet.'

The guard nods, 'It's two carriages away.'

A short time later Will stands waiting. He hears the toilet flushing and Jimmy appears from behind the door, 'Did you kill him?' says the boy.

Will frowns, 'Who?'

'The monster.'

'No.'

'Why?'

'Well, he was very strong…'

'I bet you were stronger.'

Will smiles, 'Let's get you back to your mum.'

When they get back Will stops outside the door to their compartment and peers inside. Thankfully the guard was not there, nor was the Irishman.

'Will you see the monster again?' asks Jimmy.

A chill sweeps over Will at the thought of meeting the scripture-quoting killer again, 'I hope not, Jimmy. I really hope not.'

Chapter 12

Beaulieu

The train pulls into Brockenhurst at lunchtime in a flurry of steam. Will says goodbye to Jimmy and his mum and stands up to leave. He notices the Irishman stepping on to the platform, so holds back for a moment and watches him walk toward the exit. A whistle blows and steam billows down the platform obscuring the view. Will jumps down and makes his way through the people still intent upon catching the departing train. He feels someone bump into him and turns to see the Irishman push past him. Will thinks he has been robbed. He pats his blazer pocket and breathes easy when he feels the notebook is still there.

Outside the station, it is pleasant and green, the day sunny and bright. There is no more sign of the Irishman, much to Will's relief.

He spots a battered Post Office van parked by the roadside with an old man, wearing a dirty flat cap, leaning against it and smoking a cigarette. He tips his cap with nicotine-stained fingers and bids good day to two well-dressed ladies who hurry past without acknowledging him.

Will glances up and down the road but can't see any signs for Beaulieu. He approaches the old man, 'Excuse me?'

'Afternoon, young sir.'

'Could you direct me to Beaulieu House, please?'

The man looks Will up and down, drops his cigarette to the ground and extinguishes it with his boot. 'Not many people ask to go to that place.'

Will is not sure what to say to that.

'But it just so happens I am driving in that direction.'

Will hesitates, still unsure who he can trust, 'Thank you, but I am happy to walk.'

'Well, you got a choice between a long walk, or a short drive.' The old man smiles warmly and Will thinks he has a honest face.

A fierce rumbling engine distracts him as a gleaming silver Bentley rolls slowly by. It is an Embiricos; a model that is rare and beautiful. Will realises that driving and cars are somehow familiar to him. The driver is none other than the Irishman and he is looking his way. Will's stomach clenches. He turns to the old man. 'Yes, please take me to Beaulieu, thank you.'

'Eli Pike,' says the old man, grinning. His smile is made up of a few crooked teeth and even those have seen better days.

Will hears the Embiricos' engine revving and watches with relief as it speeds away and out of sight.

'Jimmy Jones,' lies Will and extends his hand.

Eli Pike places a long bony hand in Will's. It is rough and callused. 'And this is Babs,' he says, patting the van with his other hand. 'She's a beauty, isn't she?'

'Er… yes,' says Will politely. 'Are you a postman?'

'Postman, hunter, safe cracker, Jack of all trades and master of none,' he says with a cackle and a cough. 'Right, let's get you inside.'

They drive along country roads, narrow lanes and through a small village. Eli talks casually about the war and life in the country. Will is thankful not to be pressed with personal questions.

Twenty minutes later they pull up alongside a towering wall.

Eli looks at Will, 'Are you sure you want to go there, Jimmy? We can drive on and I can drop you somewheres else.'

Eli is warning me not go to Beaulieu. Why?

Will hesitates, unsure what to say, but two men have died because of him and this notebook. Not only that, he is wanted for their murders.

It is too late for second thoughts. Besides, I have to talk to Timothy Chittlock. Only he can help me.

He must see this through, clear his name and find his parents. Beaulieu and Chittlock are his only clues to finding out what he needs. 'No thank you, Eli. Beaulieu is where I need to go.'

Eli nods once and seems disappointed with Will's answer. He points further along the road. 'See that gate just along there.'

'That's the entrance to Beaulieu House. It's locked. There is a guard standing just inside and I can tell you now, you won't get in. But, if you're interested, I have an idea.'

A few moments later Will is standing by the wall watching the van speed off. The horn blares, the brakes screech and the van swerves to a halt just outside the gate. An elderly man, a soldier from the Home Guard, emerges and shuffles toward Eli who gets out of the van and staggers around as if he is ill. The guard tries to help him. Will seizes his chance, runs to the gate and through. He glances back at Eli who winks at him.

Inside the gate, the grounds of Beaulieu are well-tended. There are gardens and scattered copses. Eli told him to follow the gravel drive, so Will does.

Beaulieu House is imposing: grey and dark with stained glass windows and a turret at each side. One turret is tall, higher than the roof, the other is shorter and looks as if it has sunk into the ground. Will approaches the front door tentatively. It is tall and wide and made from heavy dark wood. He pushes it, but it is locked. He considers knocking but decides it is best to look around and see what he is up against.

He skirts around the house, hiding behind bushes and peering through windows. He sees a dozen or so people around his age and older. Some are chatting and drinking tea, others are reading books. From behind a different bush he peers through another window. There are more young people sitting at desks watching a master who is talking to them while pointing a stick at a blueprint pinned to the wall. Will focuses. It is a diagram of a pistol. He thinks it strange that young people should be learning about pistols, but his life over the past day or so has been nothing but strange. Still, he feels uneasy.

He makes his way to the rear of the house, where he can hear people shouting in unison from somewhere on an upper floor. There is a balcony on the first floor. Its French doors are open. Inside he can make out groups of people around his age, some younger, others older, dressed in odd loose-fitting clothing like black karategi. They begin standing in pairs opposite each other. He hears someone call out an instruction and they start fighting. It is some sort of martial art, which seems strangely familiar. Their moves are mostly graceful, with the exception of a couple of students who are clunky and heavy on their feet.

Closest to the balcony is a girl with light brown hair, cut to her shoulders. Will stands transfixed. She moves with the elegance of a ballet dancer and effortlessly floors a boy twice her size. She fixes her hair behind her ears, turns and looks outside, as if bored. She sees Will and stares at him curiously. Will feels his stomach flutter.

He has lost concentration. Annoyed with himself, he turns to walk away but before he can someone grabs hold of his shoulder.

'Well, what do we have here?'

A taller boy with bright red hair is peering down at him with a look of recognition, which quickly turns to confusion then to anger.

Has he seen the sketch of me in the newspaper?

The boy is not alone. He is flanked by a large red-cheeked boy and a pinched-face girl with lank black hair hauled back and tied with a green scarf. Skulking behind them is a shorter, rounder boy with spectacles.

'Hoping to steal something, are we?' says the tall boy.

Will takes stock of him. He is slightly older than the others, around eighteen. His hair has been oiled and styled to make him seem older and his skin is pale with mountainous white-headed spots. He is wearing a smart school uniform; his navy blazer has an unusual golden crest embossed with two crisscrossed pistols and a dagger running through them.

Will edges back, his fists curling in preparation.

'We have a trespasser, Horne,' says the pinched-faced girl.

The large red-cheeked boy grabs Will from behind. Will tries to shake him off but his assailant is strong.

'Get off!'

'It speaks!' says the girl, in a mocking high-pitched voice.

Will is pulled to the ground. Horne and the pinched-face girl jump on him and pin him down.

'Check his pockets,' says Horne.

Will wrestles, kicks and spits but it is no good. There are too many of them.

Horne grabs Will's hair and raises his fist. 'Kick once more boy and I will blacken your eye.'

'I found this,' says the girl, holding up the notebook.

'Give it to me, Felicia,' says Horne.

'That's mine! Give it here!' says Will, reaching for it, but Horne just laughs and tosses the book away. The round boy with the spectacles picks it up and starts looking through it.

'Get him inside,' says Horne.

They carry Will through a side entrance. He shouts and swears, kicking out and causing one of them to cry out. They drag him into a large room and release him. Furious, Will leaps to his feet and raises his fists. His eyes dart left to right, quickly assessing his surroundings. He is standing in a great hall. Dominating the space is a stone fireplace with snout-nosed gargoyles glaring down. On the walls are heavy tapestries depicting ancient wars. Behind his captors is a wide stone staircase, which begins filling with more young people, eager to see what the commotion is. Soon Will is surrounded, trapped, his pulse racing.

The boy called Horne addresses the crowd, 'We found this trespasser spying in the grounds.'

The crowd laugh and Will feels his anger rising, his face burns.

'I say, Horne,' says the girl called Felicia, 'He looks positively feral. I shouldn't get too close.'

Horne laughs and jabs Will's still tender chest with his finger. With a mocking sneer he says, 'Apologise to the people of this school for your unwanted intrusion.'

The crowd cheer and Horne nods his appreciation, but Will pulls back his fist and launches it fast at Horne's nose. There is a sickening but satisfying crunch and Horne stumbles backward and falls onto his rump. The crowd cheers again and Will looks up to see the girl with the light brown hair on the staircase, watching him. For the briefest second he thinks he sees the trace of a smile, but she looks away with a bored expression.

The sound of a woman's voice parts the crowd, 'What the devil is going on here?'

Will turns to see a frowning woman dressed in a tweed suit.

But she is not alone.

Will's heart sinks.

Standing on one side of her is Eli Pike and, on the other side, is the Irishman from the train.

Chapter 13

The Recruit

Will's eyes dart around, searching for an escape route. Through his peripheral vision he spots Horne lunging toward him. Will is ready to strike, but Horne is pulled back by the Irishman, 'Just hold yer horses there, sonny boy. Get you and your slippery nose down to the nurse, now!'

Horne breaks free from the Irishman's grip, glares at Will and points his finger, 'We are not finished,' he says, and pushes his way through the crowd.

'Everyone back to class!' barks the Irishman.

The crowd shuffles away, murmuring and whispering. Will senses their discontentment at being robbed of the chance to see the intruder get the beating he deserves.

The round boy speaks, 'He was carrying this,' he says, handing the notebook to the squat woman in the tweed suit.

Will looks closely at the book. It looks wrong.

'A History of Bird Watching,' says the woman. She looks at him through hooded eyes, 'Did you wander in here to do a spot of bird watching?'

Realising he has been duped, Will ignores her. The Irishman must have taken the notebook and replaced it with a bird-watching book when he bumped into him at the station. Will gives him a furious stare, but the Irishman shakes his head and raises his finger to his lips. Will wants to shout at him and demand the notebook back but his instincts urge him to wait it out and say nothing.

'My name is Miss Clews, but round these parts I am known as the Major. I am the head of school. And you are?'

'Jimmy Jones,' says Will.

'Well, Mr Jones,' she says, nodding at the Irishman. 'My colleague, Eoin, tells me you've had quite the adventure breaking into our Baker Street office and making your way down to Beaulieu.'

Will frowns at the Irishman, but is secretly quite impressed. He had clearly followed him from Baker Street to Victoria. He stares back at Will, coldly.

'Come with me, please,' says the Major. She turns to Eli Pike, 'Eli, thank you.'

The old man doffs his cap and then looks at Will, 'Sorry, son.'

Will glowers at him and follows the Major, mindful that Eoin is close behind.

They walk on stone flags through hallways lit with sconces and decorated with pictures of aircraft bombers, rifles, pistols. But these are not artistic paintings or photographs, they are technical drawings whose purpose, it seems, is to educate. He wonders if this is some sort of military school. But it couldn't be, the pupils are too young to be soldiers.

The Major leads them to her office, which is a large room with maps pinned to the walls. There is a mahogany leather-topped desk and two threadbare sofas on either side of a small fireplace. On the walls are photographs of the Major. In one she is driving a racing car. In another she is standing next to a bi-plane dressed in a flying outfit complete with helmet and goggles. In another, he is surprised to see her with the Prime Minister and the royal family at a garden party. In the centre of the wall, in what seems like pride of place, she is sitting closely, hand in hand, with a tall handsome woman. They are both smiling. Will wonders if they are related but he cannot see any physical similarity.

'Please sit down,' says the Major.

Will makes his way towards one of the sofas, his eyes never leaving Eoin's. *Where is the notebook and why is he hiding it?*

'Would you like some tea?' asks the Major.

Will shakes his head and watches the Irishman walk over to the fire and pick up a poker.

His muscles tense, but the Irishman just stokes the fire.

The Major speaks, 'So, Jimmy. What is your real name?'

Will glances suspiciously from the Major to Eoin. Eoin had been carrying a newspaper on the train. He must have seen Will's face and must know he is lying. He is done for now.

'Starling. Will Starling… but I didn't kill those men!'

'The police are looking for you, so they are,' says Eoin, coolly.

'I didn't do anything. It was that Pastor, not me.'

Will notices the Major and Eoin exchanging glances.

'Describe him?' says the Major.

'I don't know who he is. I thought he was some sort of priest at first. He kept quoting the scriptures, but then he killed Skipper and Mr Batten.'

They look at Will, curiously, as if sizing him up, but say nothing.

'Why would this pastor kill those men?' says Eoin.

'I don't know. He wants something. A notebook.'

'Ah… interesting. Do you have this notebook?' says the Major.

Will glances at Eoin, whose expression is stony, 'No. Not any more.'

'Where is it?'

'He has it.'

The Irishman's eyes flash.

'Who?' says the Major.

Will hesitates. 'The Pastor.'

'Are you sure?'

'Yes. He killed those men and took it.'

The Major studies him for a moment, as if thinking over what Will has just told her. Will is not sure if she believes him.

'And what brings you to Beaulieu,' she asks.

'I'm looking for someone.'

'Who?' says the Major.

'Timothy Chittlock.'

The Major and Eoin exchange glances once again.

'Why do you wish to see him?'

Will rubs the back of his neck, unsure what to say, or how much to reveal, but what choice does he have? He needs answers. He needs to remember.

'He can help me.'

'Help you… How?'

Will swallows, rubs his thighs and looks from the Major to the Irishman. He has nothing to lose and, despite being unsure about the Irishman, he thinks the Major seems like a decent sort. It is time to come clean. He tells them everything, from the moment he woke up in the sea.

When he is finished the Major and Eoin stare at him, as if appraising him for any signs of lies.

'That's quite a story,' says Eoin at last.

'It's all true.'

'I have no doubt. But right now, I am unsure how Tim Chittlock is involved in this mystery. It may explain his present condition.'

'What do mean?' says Will.

'Tim is dead. Murdered.'

Will feels his nerves coiling. What hope is there now?

'Will you excuse us for a moment?' says Eoin. He walks with the Major to the bay window where they talk in whispers together. Moments later they return.

The Major speaks, 'Mr Starling, Eoin has made a request which I am in full agreement with. It is clear you are in danger. The men searching for you are known to us. As it happens, Eoin was on the trail of three of the men you spotted at the dockside. Do you know who they are?'

Will shakes his head.

'They are known as the agents of VIPER.'

Will shifts in his chair. The file implicating him as an agent of VIPER was on the desk in the Baker Street office. Does this mean that Eoin knows who he is? He can't tell and decides to keep quiet about it.

'Who or what is VIPER?' he asks.

'The Vendetta for International Power Estrangement and Repression are a criminal organisation with military links to almost every country in the war…'

The Major stands and, with her hands behind her back, begins pacing up and down as if deep in thought.

Will feels cold. He is part of this organisation. He is a criminal. And, if the Major and Eoin have seen the file they keep on him, they know it too, or soon will. But if he is part of VIPER, why were the men in the Austin after him?

The Major is still talking. '…They are wealthy, powerful and dangerous puppet masters whose purpose is to acquire as much power and wealth as possible though we do not know what their ultimate aims might be. They have weapons of advanced technology and most recently they have been investing their time in ancient mystical weapons related to the occult…'

Will's head begins to swim; a memory is returning. In his mind he sees a man dressed in a lab coat talking to a room full of other men. Their faces seem similar but he does not know why. There are pictures on the walls: a cluster of stones glowing blue, paintings depicting fires through the ages, the great fires of Rome and London and many more. His head begins to throb. He closes his eyes and massages his temples.

A hand grips his shoulder.

'Will, are you feeling alright? You do not look well.'

He opens his eyes and the Irishman hands him a glass of water. He drinks it and feels better immediately.

Troubled, Will pushes the memory from his mind for now. He needs to find out as much as he can.

'…That sort of mumbo-jumbo does not hold any water with me, but Eoin seems to think otherwise, and quite frankly that is good enough for me. There are many lives at stake and we need as much intelligence as we can gather to put a stop to these devils.'

'Will?' says Eoin.

'I'm fine, thank you.'

'Now,' says the Major, 'Eoin has requested you stay here until we can at least find out who you are. Hopefully we can locate your family. Are you in agreement?'

They clearly do not know who he is. Will is glad that he had the sense to remove his details from the VIPER file in Timothy Chittlock's Baker Street office. He'd be under lock and key had the Irishman got wind of where he had come from.

'Yes, thank you,' he says, relieved that he will have shelter for the time being and confused about how much the Major and Eoin know, and what they might want from him. 'What is this place?'

'It's a school.'

'What sort of school?'

'A school for spies,' says the Major, matter-of-factly.

'But the students here are young people. Some are children.'

'Spies come in all shapes, sizes and ages.'

Eoin speaks, 'Our students are a rag-tag bunch, many are orphans, with a few notable exceptions. They are all carefully selected, chosen for their intelligence, or for a particular set of talents. We shape them into unique individuals who can fit into any society, in any country, and work as part of His Majesty's Secret Service. We are the young person's branch of the Service who work alongside MI5, MI6 and the Special Operations Executive. The Prime Minister calls us the Baker Street Irregulars.'

'You will be safe here,' says the Major.

'Not to arouse suspicion,' says Eoin, 'we will enroll you as a new recruit. You will join the school and become one of us, until I find your family and understand more why VIPER and the Pastor are looking for you. How does that sound?'

The Pastor. The name sends a chill through Will's body as another piece slots into the jigsaw of his memories. It rings true to him just as his own name did when he saw it in the file. But the Pastor's name brings him no comfort at all.

Will is not convinced this place is as safe as the Major and Eoin seemed to think it is. For now, though, he needs to trust someone. He nods his head.

'Yes, I will become a recruit.'

Chapter 14

The First Night

Will follows Eoin from the Major's office to somewhere in the east wing of the house, where processing for his recruitment will begin. They stop at a door with the Irishman's name on it: *Eoin Heaney*.

The interior is sparse with wood-panelled walls and a small window. There is a desk with a row of filing cabinets behind it. These people like their files, thinks Will.

'Have a seat,' says Eoin.

Will sits at the desk and watches as Eoin begins pulling sheets of paper from one of the cabinets. He sits down opposite Will and begins writing.

'Where is my notebook?' Will says, at last.

Eoin focuses on the paperwork without looking up, 'It's safe, so it is.'

'Why did you steal it?'

'Correction: I borrowed it to protect you and the people of this school.'

'But no one knows I have it.'

'The Pastor knows you have it. VIPER know you have it. It is only a matter of time before they discover you are here. You have put us all in great danger, Mr Starling.'

Eoin's words bring home the enormity of the trouble he is in. Part of him resents the Irishman for blaming him, but the other part feels guilty. He does not want to see anyone else get hurt.

'Why did you not mention you "borrowed" the notebook to the Major?'

'As safe as Beaulieu is, these walls have ears. When the time is right, I will tell her. For now, it must remain our secret. Understood?'

Will holds his gaze but knows he has little choice in the matter. Even if he changes his mind and leaves Beaulieu with the notebook, it would only be a matter of time before the police, VIPER or the Pastor caught up with him. It would mean prison or death. Neither option would achieve anything.

Eoin passes a sheet of paper across the table. It is the Beaulieu timetable. Subjects include Espionage, Self Defence, Physical Education, Weapons, Bombs, Radio Operations, Aircraft Today, Tanks Today, Code Breaking, French, German, Latin, English, Mathematics and Honeytraps.

'There are a lot of subjects,' says Will.

'You won't need to take them all. It is more important we get you primed and ready as quickly as possible. There is little time.'

'Primed and ready?'

'We can protect you, Will. But there may come a time when you need to protect yourself. We can teach you.'

Eoin reaches into his drawer, takes out a camera and points it at him, 'Look at me,' he says. A flash of light blinds him. He blinks as Eoin concentrates on scribbling notes. Then Eoin passes across a pen and a sheet of paper with several paragraphs of printed text, 'Sign this, please.'

'What is it?'

'The Official Secrets Act. It is a requirement for all employees of His Majesty. It is to protect you and the state.'

Will signs the paper and pushes it back across the desk.

After a brief check-up with the school doctor, Will is pronounced fit for training. He follows Eoin through the great hall and down a narrow stone corridor leading to the west turret. They climb two flights of stairs and go down another corridor. Eventually Eoin stops outside a door, knocks, then steps inside. He speaks to someone for a moment then turns to Will and beckons him inside.

Will finds himself standing in a bedroom with a dresser and a wardrobe separating two bunks. Standing opposite Eoin with a terrified expression is one of Horne's friends. It is the round boy with the spectacles. On the wall, above one of the bunks, are pages of paper with illegible handwriting.

'This is your new home, Will,' says Eoin.

'But…'

Eoin turns to the round boy, 'Edward, please make our new student welcome.'

The boy called Edward does not respond, he just stares at Eoin.

'Will, this is Edward Simms, who you may remember from this afternoon.'

Will remains tight lipped, shifting awkwardly at the thought of sharing a room with one of Horne's friends.

Eoin gestures to the other bunk, 'This is yours. I will have some clothes sent up. The bathroom is across the hall. I will leave you to get to know one another. Supper is at six. Edward, be sure to show Will where the mess hall is. I think you two will become great friends.'

Eoin leaves and Edward sits gingerly on his bunk and rubs his knees. They say nothing to each other. Will ignores his new roommate and lies on the other bunk. He pushes everything from his mind, closes his eyes and breathes slowly. Tiredness overcomes him. Within minutes, he is asleep.

In his dream Will is walking blind through a mist, following the sound of a voice, a voice that is singing some sort of nursery rhyme. The mist thins and in the air before him he sees letters and numbers, some sort of code, glistening, pulsating in time to the rhyme. He tries to recognise the tune but suddenly a vast explosion melts the world around him and he hears a hundred thousand voices screaming in terror. He cries out and wakes, shivering, his face hot and clammy. Unsettled, he wonders what the meaning of the dream, but he cannot for the life of him figure it out what it might be.

The room is gloomy and he is alone. Pushing the dream from his mind, he gets out of bed and crosses to the bathroom where he splashes cold water on his face. Feeling revived, he heads downstairs in search of the mess hall.

He reaches the Great Hall, then follows the chatter and the clink of cutlery on china, which hushes to a silence when he enters the room. All eyes look his way. He stiffens and scans the room. There are four long tables with people seated randomly. Large French doors open to the gardens where adults, presumably the teachers, are chatting and smoking.

At one long table, a cook is serving up the evening meal. Will puts his head down and walks towards him. Thankfully, interest in him wanes and the chatting and clinking resumes.

Dinner turns out to be an unappealing watery grey stew. As the cook serves up, Will locks eyes with Horne who is sitting at a table in between Edward and the pinched-faced girl called Felicia. Her adoring gaze at Horne makes Will feel a little ill. Horne leans across and says something to her and she laughs. Will ignores them, grabs a spoon and napkin and sits at an empty table far away from them. As he tucks into the watery meal he feels another set of eyes watching him. He looks up to see the fighting girl from the balcony. She turns away with a haughty expression. Sitting beside her is a girl with hair the colour of butter and lips painted pillar-box red. She glances at the fighting girl and then back at Will. Then she smiles and winks. Will smiles back. She giggles and whispers something to her friend.

Instinctively, Will combs his hair with his fingers and thinks he might introduce himself later.

An Irish accent interrupts Will's thoughts, 'Not exactly the Ritz but it's the best we can do during war time,' says Eoin, pulling up a chair.

'How long do you think I have to be here?'

'That depends.'

'On what?'

'On you.'

'But…'

'Be patient, Will. There is much to be done. For now, I need you to be as fit as a soldier, never mind a spy. Training begins tomorrow.'

'What sort of training?'

'You will see.' Eoin passes him a sheet of paper.

It is a detailed floor plan of Beaulieu House.

'The rooms circled in red are where they teach the classes I want you to take. We are midway through the school year, and the others will be ahead of you. Do not concern yourself with that. I have briefed the teachers and allowances will be made. You will need to work hard to catch up.'

Will looks closely at the map. There are rooms labelled: Weapons, Espionage, Radio Operations, Physical Training and Self Defence.

As if reading his mind Eoin says, 'You'll get used to it, so you will.'

Will's thoughts turn to the dream about codes and the rhyme, 'I had a dream – there were clues. I'd like to see the notebook. I think I might be able to interpret what some of the text means.'

Eoin regards him curiously. 'Let's concentrate on your training first,' he says, standing up. 'That is your priority. I will see you in the morning, Will. Goodnight.'

Back in his room, Will lies back on his bunk, curiosity about the notebook clawing away at his mind.

Why is it coded? What is it concealing? Why are dangerous people prepared to kill anyone to get it?

In the dream he had heard hundreds of thousands of voices screaming in terror. It has left him feeling cold inside.

There's a movement outside. The doorknob turns once, then stops. Will swings out of bed, his eyes flit around the room looking for something he can use as a weapon, but whoever was there has walked on by.

He peeks through the door and up the hallway. The bathroom light is on and he can hear water running. He slides across the hall and peers inside. Edward is bent over a washbasin, shaking. His broken spectacles are resting on the side of the basin. There is blood splashed over the sink's white enamel. Will goes in and looks at him side on. His top lip is split and his left eye is red and swollen. There are dried tears on his cheeks.

'Leave me alone,' he croaks.

'Who did this?' demands Will.

Edward does not respond, but he doesn't need to. Will is sure it was Horne.

'Let me help you,' he says, picking up a towel. He runs cold water on it, folds it over and places it against Edward's swollen eye, 'Hold this.'

Edward does not protest. He turns and sits on the edge of one of the bathtubs, his hand pressing down on the wet towel, 'I'm going to get into so much trouble,' he says.

'Why?'

But Edward gazes at the floor and does not respond.

'I can take you to the medical room, if you like.'

Edward shakes his head.

'Horne did this, didn't he?'

Edward looks away without saying yes or no.

'You should tell Eoin or the Major.'

Edward shakes his head. Will does not push it. He knows there is an unwritten rule in every school that you do not snitch. Snitching usually results in more beatings and sometimes a lot worse.

'He can't get away with this.'

'He gets away with a lot worse. His family are wealthy and have influence.'

'But I thought everyone here was an orphan.'

'Not everyone. Did the Major not tell you about the "few notable exceptions"?'

'Yes, I remember. But I wasn't quite sure what it meant.'

'Now you know.'

Edward peels the towel from his eye. Will takes it from him and rings it through with more cold water before handing it back.

'Thank you,' says Edward.

Will shrugs. 'You should get some sleep.'

Will turns to leave.

'He wants me to spy on you. He wants to know why you are here and being treated with such importance.'

Will feels his hackles rising and snorts. *Importance?* He almost wants to tell Edward about the attempts on his life and the two men who were killed because of him, but he holds his tongue. The less people know the better. For the time being at least.

'He says I am to blame this on you. But I won't. I hate him.'

'Tell people you fell over, and stay as far away from Horne as you can. I can handle him and his friends.'

Edward manages a half smile.

'Let's get you back to the room.' Will helps him up, 'You'll have a proper shiner in the morning. You wait.'

Chapter 15

Assembly

Will wakes the next morning to someone calling his name. Wiping the sleep from his eyes he looks up to see Eoin standing at the foot of his bunk. In one arm he is holding clothes, in the other is a battered leather satchel.

'I did knock but there was no answer.'

'What time is it?'

'7 am. There is an assembly at 8 am, in the Great Hall. Make sure you are there.'

Eoin drops the clothes onto the bed. 'Your uniform, and training kit. There are textbooks and everything else you need for lessons in the bag. Bring it and your training kit with you.' And with that, Eoin leaves the room.

Will heaves himself out of bed and hears Edward just beginning to stir beneath the covers.

The pile of clothes includes a red and blue striped tie, a navy blazer with the bronze criss-crossed pistol and dagger crest, a blue shirt, a grey jumper and dark tweed trousers; the standard issue uniform for Beaulieu, it seems. There is also a pair of shorts, a vest and plimsoles.

He picks up the blazer and slides his hand along the lining of the sleeves and wonders if they have any hidden tools like his other blazer. There are none. He wonders again why he would have such a blazer. Who would have tailored something like that to house those kinds of tools? He thinks about the photographs at the Baker Street office. Was he really an enemy agent for the Agents of VIPER?

I can't be. I would never betray my country.

Or would he? Did he have reason to? The thought makes him go cold. He has no memories, nothing concrete to cling to. All he knows is the Agents of VIPER and some mad pastor are trying to kill him, and he has something they both want. He peers out the window – the gardens are misty and damp and look cold for the time of year. He rubs his arms and gets dressed.

The Great Hall is alive with the laughter and voices of students. He sees Horne, Felicia and the large boy glowering at him and imagines they are appalled to see him in their precious Beaulieu uniform. He levels his gaze at Horne and smiles a half smile, watching with satisfaction as Horne stiffens, his face burning red. His spots look like they are about to explode.

He notices the crests on the student blazers vary in colour: most are silver and bronze. Only Horne appears to wear a golden badge.

'It suits you,' says a voice.

Will turns to see the girl with the butter hair and painted red lips.

'Erm… thanks,' says Will.

She smiles and extends her hand, 'I'm Violet.'

Her hand is soft and warm. 'Will.'

'I know. Everyone knows who you are.'

Will is a little surprised to hear that. 'They do?'

'Oh yes. We're all speculating like mad on why you are here. I know we shouldn't. Top secret and all that, but who doesn't like a bit of gossip.'

Will opens his mouth to speak but does not know what to say.

Violet continues, 'You must meet my friend. She's dying to get to know you.'

'Violet!' says a voice.

Violet turns and pulls someone from behind her. It is the fighting girl from the balcony. She seems furious.

Will notices that she and Violet have silver crests.

'Will, meet Anna Wilder,' says Violet, shoving Anna forward.

Anna Wilder pushes back. Her cheeks flush with indignation. Then she turns and storms off into the crowd. Will does not know what to make of her. Snooty seems like a good description.

Violet shrugs. 'Don't mind her. She'll come around.'

Will has no idea what she will come around to and changes the subject, 'Why are the crests different colours?'

'A bronze crest is for new students, those wet behind the ears so to speak,' she says with a wink. 'Silver is awarded to those who have successfully completed their training and their first mission. Gold is awarded to those outstanding students who have three successful missions under their belt. There is only one golden crest in the school and that belongs to Horne.'

Violet makes a vomiting gesture and leans toward Will conspiratorially, 'Some of us know the truth about Horne. Successful missions – I don't think so. Family connections got him the gold.'

Will is distracted when Eoin and the Major appear at the foot of the staircase. They are accompanied by several other adults, presumably schoolmasters.

The Major is talking to a slender man with a wide serious face and a long hook-like nose.

'That master talking to the Major is Nicholas Morrow. MI6,' says Violet. 'Slippery fellow, if you ask me.'

Next to him is a taller lady with a dreamy expression and a whistle round her neck. It is the handsome woman from the picture in the Major's office. Standing next to her is an Indian gentleman wearing a vivid green turban.

'And that's Miss Davenport, who teaches games and physical training. Mr Singh is Communications and Code Breaking.'

The Major stands on the stairs and faces the crowd, 'Good morning,' she says loudly.

The crowd continue to chatter, seemingly oblivious. She raises her arms and drops them slowly in a hushing motion, but no one seems to notice.

She rolls her eyes and nods politely to the tall lady with the whistle. The masters cover their ears as she blows hard.

The chatter dwindles and fades to a whisper and then complete silence.

The Major nods her thanks and turns to the students. 'Good morning all.'

'Good morning,' the students mumble in unison.

The Major smiles and then her expression turns grave. 'In the last few days the Germans have walloped London and Coventry. There are many casualties and far too many deaths.' She pauses for a moment, in thought, before continuing. 'There are occupying forces in the Netherlands and we also know that, in the next few days, Paris will be taken. The Third Reich is spreading across Europe like a tumour.'

There is a grumbling from the students and Will senses a feeling of unease. He thinks it odd that in just over twenty-four hours he has come to terms with the war. It is part and parcel of this cold and dangerous existence he has woken up to.

'…Never has the work of this school been more vital to the war effort. Your commitment and bravery will go down in history, which is why we must continue to learn and become the best at what we do.'

A rumble of agreement ripples through the crowd.

The Major gestures at Nicolas Morrow. 'Some of you will know Mr Morrow. He is here to assess certain students for a posting at MI6. So please, do your best to impress.'

There is a murmur of excitement from the crowd.

The Major continues, 'The war is not abating, it is building. The Army, the Navy, the Air Force all need new recruits and so do we. I am always on the lookout for new talent and today I would like to introduce you to a new addition to the school.'

Will stiffens.

'I would ask you – no, I will tell you – to forget what you saw yesterday and welcome our new student, Will Starling.'

Will squirms inside as all heads turned to look at him.

He does not react to the gaze of the many curious eyes, but he can feel one pair in particular boring into him from the foot of the staircase. He turns to see Nicholas Morrow, frowning at him.

'Will is going to undertake a fast-track training program with Mr Heaney as his mentor,' says the Major. 'So please, make him feel welcome.'

Everyone claps with the exception of Horne and his friends.

'Righto, everyone. It's almost 8.15 am and another school day begins,' says the Major, rubbing her hands together.

The boys' changing room is narrow, bare and cold, with a single row of grubby wooden benches dividing the limited floor space. Will stands among the bustle of boys, his nose wrinkling at the sour stench of unwashed bodies. There are suspicious glances and whispers in his direction. It is unsettling, but he is well aware that he is a stranger and, to some, an unwelcome outsider.

However, none of that concerns him. He has greater things to worry about. He drops his kit on the bench and removes his blazer, tie and shirt. He feels a shove from behind and stumbles forward banging his knee on the bench. There is laughter. He turns to see Horne's spotty face looking down at him. With him is the large boy who had floored Will from behind yesterday. He towers over him like some sort of giant with a red face and pink pudgy fists.

'Have you run many cross-country courses, Starling?' says Horne, in a mocking tone.

Will rubs his knee and bristles. He has no memory of running any courses. 'I'm sure if you can do it, it can't be difficult.'

Horne raises his arms in a theatrical gesture and addresses the boys. 'Observe how our new recruit brims with confidence.'

Laughter erupts.

Horne glares at Will and points at the crest on his blazer, 'I am the only gold in this school. Do not forget that.'

Will's hands curl into fists. He could take both of them out easily, in less than seven seconds by his calculation. Horne has made a mistake already by being too close. A knee in the groin would disable him and before his knees hit the ground, Will's fist would be gracing the giant's nose. Seven seconds. No more. Easy.

His heart begins to beat faster. A primal urge for violence surges through him. He so wants to teach these amateurs a lesson. They have it coming.

And then Horne leans forward, his face is so close Will almost gags on his stale breath. 'It takes even the fittest person four weeks before they can complete this course. I am cross-country champion. You are…' Horne looks Will up and down, '…nothing.'

Horne snorts and then walks to the other end of the changing room. The giant lingers to glare at Will through small button-like eyes.

'Sneddon!' barks Horne.

The large boy flinches and backs away, jabbing a thick digit in the air at Will.

Will is relieved they have gone. His self-control was about to be tested but, lucky for those two, it wasn't. He checks himself. His desire to hurt those two boys makes him shudder.

Who am I? What am I?

He is confident that in time he will know the answers to those questions but for now he must keep a low profile and not draw attention to himself by being rash and stupid. He glances over at the two boys.

That does not mean, however, that I cannot have some fun.

Chapter 16

The Race

Will makes his way to the front of Beaulieu House where the cross-country runners are gathering. It begins to spot with rain and goosebumps prickle his skin. The girls, including Violet, Anna and Horne's friend Felicia are waiting. Despite the morning being cold and dull, there is an excited hum in the air.

Eoin stands at the front of the crowd, 'Start warming up,' he calls and begins jogging on the spot. 'I want you to put everything you have into today's race. Forget your aching muscles. Forget the stitch in your side. Forget your gasping lungs. Run like your life depends on it. Because one day, it will.'

A grim silence hangs over the crowd.

More rain begins to fall. Will looks upwards. Thick grey clouds are rolling across the sky like giant sheep. A feeling of déjà vu unsteadies him; a memory flashes into his mind: a rainy day in a remote and treacherous landscape. He is wearing dark green fatigues. There are others like him but bigger, older, with shaven heads. He knows them, but not their names. A voice is booming at them – a stern, angry voice. They are running across fields, up hills and mountainsides with heavy boots thumping on the coarse, uneven terrain. It is relentless and unforgiving.

'Will!'

Will snaps out of his fug and sees the others running into the distance. Eoin is looking back at him, beckoning him to hurry. Will swears under his breath and springs after them, troubled by the memory.

He catches up with Eoin, who points to a wooded area in the distance. 'We're running through those woods, then along the river and across to the assault course. We'll meet back here. It's your first time, so do your best and try not to get lost.'

Eoin runs off in pursuit of the others.

Still spooked by the memory, Will lags behind, his performance hindered by a blurred sense of reality. *Who am I?* He rubs his head and feels the gash on his temple under this thick hair. It is still tender. The pain jolts him and he feels foolish. He looks ahead and tries to see where everyone is, but it is misty and the view is obscured. He increases his pace, breathing slowly through his nose and mouth, exhaling in time to the rhythm of his running.

He hears the crunching of twigs and turns to see a boy he doesn't recognise leaping over a wire fence and disappearing into the woods. Will runs at the fence, leaps over it and sprints after him. The ground is uneven and slippery. Thick clustered trees slow him down. He runs for twenty minutes with no sighting of the boy or anyone else. He stops to get his bearings and catch his breath. He has a stitch in his side and his muscles burn with the exertion.

'No resting!' shouts Eoin from somewhere beyond the trees. Will focuses on the direction of his voice and runs toward it. Although he cannot see him, he can hear the Irishman's fast and heavy footfalls and follows in their wake.

He estimates fifteen minutes has passed before he clears the woods and catches sight of Eoin and the others. They are running uphill, alongside a river. He sees Anna and Violet amongst the melee following Horne, who is way ahead of everyone.

Will steadies his breathing and takes measured sprints toward the crowd. Trailing behind them is the burly Sneddon, who glances back at him. He is red faced and struggling to get up the hill. Will passes him, narrowly missing a podgy pink fist swiping close to his face. He almost laughs but runs on passing three more boys and Felicia.

He runs for twenty minutes along the bank against the current and stops at what seems the most dangerous part. The water is swirling furiously, drowning out any other sound. Will watches as the others wade through the waist-high treacherous rapids. Beside him are Anna and Violet. They work as a team and hold on to each other as they step down. Will follows, but someone shoves him and he falls against Anna. They both topple over. Will swallows a mouthful of grey, gritty water as the undertow drags him downstream. He swims to the top and grabs hold of an old uprooted tree jutting overhead. Anna surfaces beside him, gasping for breath, her hair sodden and plastered to her face.

'Grab my hand!' calls Will.

Anna grips his arm and Will guides them out of the water and onto the muddy bank.

'What the hell do you think you are doing?' she shouts.

'I just saved you!'

'You've just cost me this race!'

Will opens his mouth to explain but Anna has is already making her way back down to the river. She wades across to the other side where Violet waits. Will can almost feel the steam coming out of his ears, and turns his attention to whoever pushed him. Felicia is the only one nearby. She smiles slyly, before hurrying up the bank and back into the race.

Will wades carefully through the water and hauls himself up the riverbank, plodding through the thick mud. He picks up his pace as the ground grows firmer and assesses what lies ahead. The runners are sprinting towards a wall that looks like a great brick slab plonked in the middle of the countryside. It is approximately fifteen foot wide and twenty foot tall. It is less than quarter of a mile ahead, perhaps one thousand feet. If he runs uninterrupted, he could make it in three minutes, maybe less. He inhales and exhales, filling his lungs with oxygen, and springs forward.

The runners are spread out. Felicia glances back at him, but Will ignores her. He can see Violet and Anna following in the tracks of Horne who is still leading, and almost halfway to the wall. Will hurries forward and breaks into a sprint. Like a hound pursuing a fox, he focuses on Horne and pounds across the field.

Now is my time to have fun.

Felicia turns to face him, raising her arms like some sort of goalkeeper trying to prevent him from getting to the back of the net, but Will runs wide and skims past her. He overtakes several more runners and sees five ropes hanging down from the wall. Horne, Violet and Anna are almost there and leap across a pool of water at the foot of the wall. They begin climbing the ropes.

Will leaps across the small pool like a long-jump athlete and reaches for the thick rope, but he slams against the wall, his hands gripping desperately, his knuckles grazed and bleeding against the rough bricks. The rope is slippery. It is difficult to maintain purchase. He tightens his grip and pulls with all his strength, but he keeps inching further down. He grits his teeth and holds on, but the rain crashes down, hampering his efforts. He blinks and tries to look above but the water stings his eyes. He wipes them with his forearm and sees Horne almost at the top. Anna and Violet are close behind but are struggling against the downpour. Their technique is poor, with limbs wrapped around the rope, they haul their weight slowly up. In this weather, there is a better way to climb a slippery rope. Using one foot, Will catches the rope and with the other he creates a loop. He is then able to stand on the rope with ease and haul himself upwards.

He is close to the top when he sees a shadow looming directly above him. Horne is crouched, watching him like a hyena stalking its prey. Will hesitates, suspicious. He glances down and swallows, his throat dry. If he slips, or there is an *accident*, he could be done for. He steadies his breathing and carries on climbing, his eyes never leaving Horne's. He reaches forward, his fingers gripping the ledge. Horne stands up and raises his foot. He presses it down on Will's fingers. The pain is unbearable. He hears Violet shouting at Horne to stop, but his strength is sapping, he can't keep his grip and then he falls. Scrambling for purchase, Will clings to the slippery rope, his hands and legs burning with the friction. Eventually, he stops his slide and looks up to see Felicia hopping over the edge. Violet and Anna are looking down from the top. Violet is waving her arms, shouting for him to climb up.

Will is sodden, his muscles ache, the skin on his hands and legs feels like it is on fire. He wants to cry out, but he won't let himself. He must not give up. Ignoring the pain, he climbs back to the top.

Violet and Anna have already taken off. He can see Eoin in the distance beside a row of monkey bars, gesturing at everyone to hurry. Horne is ahead; Felicia, Violet and Anna are following close behind. He looks quickly at his hands. The skin is hanging off. He removes his vest, tears it in two and wraps the material around his palms and fingers. He slides quickly down the rope. His feet hit the ground lightly and he springs forward. Breathing through his mouth and nose, he increases his pace and soon flies past Felicia, who shouts some obscenity at him.

Horne is crossing the monkey bars with Anna and Violet inches behind him. Will leaps onto them, wincing at the pain in his hands, but thankful they are protected with his ripped vest.

Horne, Anna and Violet are neck and neck, heading toward what look like shallow underground tunnels. Horne crawls into one; Violet and Anna dip into the other.

Will drops off the bars and hurries toward the tunnels. He dives into the tunnel behind Horne. There is no light. It is cold and wet with an earthy smell, like a long empty grave. He can hear Horne squelching through the mud. Will tries to catch him up but his hands and knees sink in the quagmire, slowing his progress. He pulls them out and lies down on his front with his arms and legs flat, crawling across the surface of the mud, ignoring the stones and wood that scrape his bare chest. He should be spent, but a fire burns in him and he carries on.

But then something tugs at his foot. It is a hand. Felicia! Will pulls his foot away, freeing from the grip but losing a plimsole at the same time. Felicia grabs him again. She is strong, but he pulls his foot free and crawls fast toward the opening where the back of Horne's head is framed.

Horne is out of the tunnel. Seconds later Will emerges and sees him disappear into a copse of trees. The rain lashes down, washing the mud from his tired body.

Eoin is ahead, calling to Will. 'Well done, lad. Faster. You are almost there!'

Will runs through the copse, zigzagging around trees and jumping over rocks. Through the woods, he sees Horne and beyond him, Beaulieu House. He dashes forward and clears the copse. It is open land now all the way to Beaulieu. He sprints downhill. In seconds he is level with Horne. He can see a stream approaching and launches himself at it. The water is deeper than expected. Horne is beside him now, his expression grim and determined. Will pulls himself to the other side, ignoring the pain in his bare foot from the scraps of wood and gravel.

He can see some of pupils outside the school watching and cheering them on. The Major and Morrow are there too, looking on with interest.

Will pushes on. Horne is beside him again, inching his body forward to get ahead but Will calls on his last reserves of energy and forces himself in front. Will skids to a stop close to Morrow and drops to his knees on the grass, gasping for breath. There is an almighty cheer.

'Bravo, Starling,' says the Major.

'Good work, Will!' says Eoin.

'Thank you,' says a breathless Will. Horne manages to look both furious and confused. Will smiles, happy to have beaten him, but still he cannot help wonder what the boy's problem is.

'Impressive, Starling,' says a tinny voice.

Morrow is watching him through narrowed eyes. 'I will be keeping a watchful eye on you.'

There is something about Morrow that sets Will on edge. He cannot quite put his finger on it.

Violet and Anna arrive. They congratulate him and Violet gives him a warm hug, much to Anna's apparent surprise. She still keeps her distance, although twice he catches her looking furtively at his muddy, bare torso.

Chapter 17

Spy School

Will showers and very soon feels like a different person. To his satisfaction, Horne and Sneddon leave the changing room without any fuss. They can see he is clearly not the soft target they had anticipated.

Using Eoin's map of Beaulieu house, Will navigates the corridors, looking for his first class: Radio Operations. According to the map it should be on the first floor. He crosses the Great Hall, hurries up the staircase, turns right and stops outside the second door on the left. He places his ear to it and hears Mr Singh talking.

He knocks twice and steps inside.

'Ah, William. I've been expecting you. Please join us,' says Mr Singh.

Will closes the door and glances around the room. There are six tables in rows of two. Each table has a suitcase on top. Seated around each one are three students. Will can see familiar faces including Violet, Anna and Horne with his two idiot friends. There is one table with a single student, sporting a large back shiner on his left eye.

'Please, sit with Edward,' says Mr Singh.

Will hesitates, but heads toward the table. He can see Edward go rigid.

'Relax, Edward,' he says, glancing at Horne whose eyes dart from Edward to Will. Something in Horne's frown tells Will that the plan to get him into trouble has backfired. Will winks at him and Horne scowls.

'Open up your communications devices, please,' says an enthusiastic Mr Singh.

Edward unfastens the clasps and opens the lid of the case. The smell of fresh wood polish fills Will's nostrils. Inside is a gleaming new radio communications set built neatly into the suitcase. There is a compartment containing the headphones, a large rectangular power pack and a panel with dials and buttons that operates the transmitter and the receiver.

'It's a Whaddon Mark VII,' says Will.

'Yes, it is,' says Edward.

He can feel Edward looking at him.

'How do you know that?'

Will shifts uneasily. 'Erm… a lucky guess.'

The radio has an unsettling familiarity to it, as if he has seen or used one before. Will listens attentively to Mr Singh, ignoring Edward's curious gaze.

By the end of the class, Edward has warmed up and they have even managed to exchange a few more words. He feels the beginnings of a bond, although it is still fragile.

The following morning, Will attends the Deadly Gadgets class taught by Eoin. The Irishman demonstrates a range of weird devices such as time pencils for detonating explosives, nitrate paper that explodes on contact with flames and bombs disguised as clockwork rats.

'Wind them up and watch them scurry toward their target,' says Eoin.

Will can not resist winding up a fake rat bomb and sending it toward Horne and his henchmen. He has never seen anyone move so fast. The class roars with laughter.

Later, Will attends Self-Defence, which is taught by the tall, athletic Miss Davenport. Her class is held in the gymnasium, a vast ornate room on the first floor that looks like it had once been a ballroom. It is the place where Will first saw Anna. Across the room he sees her standing comfortably in her loose-fitting black karategi. He watches her for a moment, transfixed, before Miss Davenport speaks.

'Righto, everyone. Today is Will's first self-defence lesson. As you know, self-defence is key to survival. Therefore, no kid gloves in this class,' she gives a guffawing laugh.

Will notices some students rolling their eyes.

Miss Davenport continues, 'Will, pretend I am a ruthless Nazi killer stalking her prey. You are an undercover agent in possession of secret information that is key to saving hundreds of lives. We will fight to the death,' she says. 'I will be gentle,' she adds, but Will swears her eyes have taken on a canine quality.

Out of the corner of his eye, Will sees someone entering the room. It is Eoin, who stands out of the way watching.

Miss Davenport turns to face Will, her fists raised in attacking mode, '*Schweinhund!*' she bellows in a mock German accent. Will ignores the giggles from the class and watches as Miss Davenport's fist flies toward him. He leans to the left, the fist narrowly missing his ear. Miss Davenport throws several more punches, swipes and kicks but he dodges every single one.

Will watches her, determining what she will do next. It isn't that she is a terrible fighter; she is fast and skilled, but he seems to be able to anticipate her every move by reading her body language. How on earth can he know this? The answer makes him feel cold. But deep down he has known since he saw the file in Baker Street.

I'm one of them. I'm an agent of VIPER.

Miss Davenport tries her best but cannot quite hit her target. Minutes later, puffed out and red-faced, Miss Davenport relents, 'Very good, Will. Clearly you have done this before.'

'No, Miss, this is my first time.' What else could he say?

The class giggle again.

He glances at Eoin who is still watching him.

Miss Davenport looks despondent. 'Oh… Maybe I'm losing my touch,' she says.

'No… you were very good,' says Will.

'Really?' she says, smiling.

'Really.'

Miss Davenport turns and looks across the gym, her expression clouding over. 'Good Lord, what is that?' she says.

Will tenses and looks, but before he can see what it is his legs are kicked from under him. He falls to the mat, his arm in a vice-like grip and Miss Davenport's knees pinning down his chest.

'Ha!' she cries. 'Never let your guard down in front a murderous Nazi, Will.'

The class erupts in laughter and, despite his shock, Will laughs too, which injects in him a sudden surge of hope.

Perhaps I'm not one of them. Perhaps I'm a good person.

Miss Davenport addresses the class. 'Break into twos and press on!' She stands up, takes Will's arm and helps him up. 'Sorry, old boy,' she says.

Will shakes his head. He can't help liking Miss Davenport and her passion. 'I let my guard down. You win.'

'I'm impressed, Will. Your non-contact avoidance of my attack was highly skilled. I find it hard to believe you have not had lessons before this.'

Will looks away and says nothing more, relieved that she doesn't press him further. He looks to Eoin and sees him leave quietly, shutting the door behind him.

Chapter 18

Shooting Class

Thursday, 8th May 1941

Will wakes with a sense of urgency. His muscles are tight and the throb in his temple has returned like a visceral warning for him to get moving. More than twenty-four hours have passed since he saw Eoin leave Miss Davenport's Self-Defence class. He senses that the Irishman has left Beaulieu. Could this be an opportunity to search for the notebook? It must be hidden somewhere in the school. As soon as he has the idea, he dismisses it. Beaulieu is vast and it could take him weeks, if not months.

He feels that he has very little time, though where this thought has come from he can't say. What he does know is that he must find the notebook.

He makes his way to the Major's office to find out if she knows where Eoin is.

'You'll find him at the shooting range, where I believe you have your next lesson, Mr Starling,' she says, quickly peering up at him through half-moon spectacles.

The distraction of the notebook had made him forget his lessons. 'Erm... I apologise for disturbing you, Major. I'll go there immediately.'

'Righto. Hurry along then. You are already a trifle late.'

Will hurries through the grounds and hears the sound of a gunshot. The class has already begun. He runs through a copse and sees Eoin standing next to a table with a holdall on top of it. In his hand is a pistol. He is talking to a group of students. Among them he sees Anna, Violet, Horne and his crew. Eoin looks up as Will approaches and then all eyes turn in Will's direction.

'You're late, Starling.'

'Sorry, sir.'

Horne and his friends huddle together and giggle. Will ignores them and looks toward the targets, which are a row of six faceless scarecrows stuffed with straw and dressed in patched-up suits and hats.

'For the benefit of Starling, a quick recap,' says Eoin. He holds up a pistol. 'This is the Webley Mark IV, British made and standard issue. It is a revolver. Can anyone tell me what makes it a revolver?'

Will opens his mouth to answer, but Horne speaks up first.

'It's…' starts Horne but is interrupted by Eoin.

'Hand please, Horne.'

Horne's neck reddens and he slowly raises his hand, 'Sir?'

'Yes, Horne.'

'A revolver is a repeating firearm that has a revolving cylinder containing multiple chambers and one barrel for firing. The term "revolver" refers to a handgun, but other weapons may also have a revolving chamber. These include some models of …'

Eoin cuts Horne short. 'Thank you, Horne, we get the idea.' He opens the holdall. Inside are several more Webley revolvers. 'Partner up and take one pistol between two of you.'

Will looks around. There are several boys including Horne hovering around Violet and Anna, hoping to partner and show off with them. He notices Violet looking his way. She glances wickedly at Anna. 'Anna and Will are shooting together!' she calls to Eoin.

'Very good,' says Eoin. 'Anna, please help Will.'

Will sees Anna's face burning red. Violet winks at Will and he frowns. *What is Violet playing at?*

Anna makes her way through the crowd and stands next to Will without looking at him.

'Have you used a gun before,' she asks, haughtily.

Will glances at the bag of guns and says nothing. Part of him is repelled at these tools of death, but part of him is also excited about the opportunity to know what it is like to hold and shoot a gun. But there is something else. Something at the edge of his memory.

Anna puffs and shakes her head.

Will suspects she thinks he is a little afraid. He frowns, his patience with this stuck-up girl is fading fast. He wants to say something clever when he notices Horne. He is gripping his Webley and glaring in Will's direction. Will wouldn't be surprised if he tried to put a bullet in him and claim it as an accident.

Eoin walks through the crowd handing out boxes the size of a small fist. They contain bullets.

'Load the bullets and take aim at your target,' demands Eoin. 'Point your gun at the scarecrows and get ready for my signal.'

'Watch what I do,' says Anna. 'Point the barrel away from you toward the ground.'

Will watches as Anna flicks a switch at the side the gun. 'It's a top-break revolver. This switch unlocks the gun.' She pushes the barrel down, revealing the chamber.

Will takes six bullets from the box and hands them across. Although still irritated by her, he watches with admiration as Anna's slender hands skilfully load the bullets and lock the gun back into place.

Six students including Anna, Violet and Horne stand at the frontline.

'Aim!' bellows Eoin. He walks behind each one of them, checking their positions. He stops beside Violet. 'Steady your aim, Violet.'

'It's too heavy,' she says.

'Then support your gun hand with your other arm.' Eoin takes the gun from her and points it toward the targets. He cups his free hand under his gun hand and looks back at her. 'Like so.'

He walks to the top of the line, gives one final check and shouts, 'Fire!'

Will covers his ears. The air is filled with deafening blasts.

Anna's and Horne's scarecrows shudder, their straw filled arms flap life-lessly in a sinister dance as their bullets hit their marks.

'Good work, Miss Wilder and Horne. The rest of you need more practice. Pass the guns to your partner.'

Anna hands the Webley to Will. It is heavy and warm to the touch. His fingers curl around it and hold it with an unsettling confidence. He trembles and feels a wave of dizziness pass over him.

'Look at Starling's face!' laughs Horne. 'Are you frightened?'

A surge of anger rushes through Will.

'Don't listen to him,' says Anna. 'Concentrate.'

Will takes three deep breaths and focuses. He recalls Anna's instruction but there is something else. He knows what he is doing. Pointing the barrel at the ground, he opens it and slowly inserts the bullets into the chamber. He takes up his position at the frontline.

'Aim!' says Eoin.

Will's gun is stiff and difficult to lock. He fiddles with it clumsily until it gives way and closes. He pushes the barrel up, locking it in place. He aims, the gun is heavy and wobbles for a moment before he steadies it.

'Fire!'

Will flinches as the gunshots ring out. He squeezes the trigger but nothing happens.

'Starling?' says Eoin.

He hears sniggering from the other students but ignores it. The trigger is jammed. He slams the gun with the palm of his hand without really knowing why. Something clicks. Supporting the gun hand with his free hand, he aims the Webley at the scarecrow, one eye staring down the top of the barrel and over the sight. His stomach is in knots, but he breathes slowly.

His arm is steady; the sight is aimed directly at the scarecrow's heart.

He squeezes the trigger firing off six rounds without flinching. Dust flies from the scarecrow, its arms flailing in a vain protest as the bullets thud one by one into its straw chest.

Will swallows. He has hit the target with each bullet.

There is silence; no one speaks.

He hears a creaking sound and watches as the scarecrow flops forward and falls to the ground, a twisted and lifeless straw corpse.

His mouth dries. For a moment he thinks he has been lucky, but he knows this is not the case. Moments back there was something he could not quite fathom. He understands now what that was – he knows how to fire a gun. Confused, he shudders and again wonders who he really is. He trembles and lowers the Webley downwards.

There is a cheer from the other students.

He looks around to see them closing in around him, slapping his back and congratulating him.

All except Horne and his crew.

Will's mood lifts instantly as he laps up the sudden praise. He glances at Eoin who is regarding him with an unreadable expression.

'That's all for today,' says Eoin. 'Place the guns in the bag on the table. I will be counting them.'

'Nice work,' says Violet.

'Thanks,' says Will and looks at Anna.

'You are full of surprises, aren't you?' she says, folding her arms.

He looks away. She is right to be curious.

The class begins to disperse.

'Will,' says Eoin. 'Come to my office. I need to talk to you.'

'Yes, of course.'

Eoin nods, hands him the bag containing the guns and together they walk back to the school.

Chapter 19

Languages

Will is standing in Eoin's office watching him lock the bag of pistols into a steel cabinet. The Irishman has said nothing since they left the firing range.

'How many languages can you speak?' he says at last.

Confused by the question, Will frowns, 'Just English.'

Eoin nods. 'You did well today,' he says, changing the subject.

'It was just luck,' says Will, folding his arms.

Eoin snorts, 'Is that what it was?'

'Yes!'

'And you also got lucky during Self-Defence?'

Will swallows and fails to answer.

The Irishman looks at him with an inquisitive stare. 'You've never fired a gun before? Not once?'

'I was lucky, that's all.' But Will feels a nervous tingling in his stomach and knows Eoin is not convinced by his answers.

'Perhaps you are right,' says Eoin.

But Will sees the doubt in his eyes. He frowns at the Irishman, 'Why don't you believe me?' he snaps.

'I did not say that I don't believe you.'

'But you don't, do you? You think I'm a liar!'

'No I don't. I just think you are confused.'

'What does that mean?'

'It means I think there's more to you than we think.'

'So you do think I'm lying?'

'I didn't say that.'

'But it's what you meant.'

'Not exactly.'

'Then why don't you just say what you mean?' Will's anger is at tipping point. Suddenly, the events of the last few days hit him hard and he cannot contain his patience any longer. He wants to let rip and get everything off his chest, but Eoin turns casually away and looks out the window. 'Thank you, Will.'

Will's hands curl into fists. 'Is that it? Is that all you have to say?' He desperately wants to kick something but turns and heads for the door.

'*Ich habe nicht gesagt dass Sie gehen können!*' says Eoin.

Will stops, his heart pounding, his hand grips the doorknob hard. *I did not say you could leave.*

'*Tout n'est pas fini entre nous,*' says Eoin.

Will trembles. *I'm not finished with you.* Eoin had just spoken in German and French and he had understood every word.

'Sit down, Will.'

For a moment he feels paralysed and unable to move from the door. But then a warm hand rests on his shoulder and Eoin guides him to a chair. Will does not protest. He sits down, his mind a flurry of confusion. He hears the sound of liquid pouring and suddenly there is a glass of water in front of him.

'Drink this.'

Will drinks slowly, one sip, then two, before downing the lot. It makes him feel a little better, 'I… I don't understand what is happening to me.'

'Don't try to yet.'

'But I have to know. I feel like I'm a stranger in my own body.'

'You're not. Trust me.'

Will looks at Eoin with a sense of hope. 'What happened to me? How did I get to this point?'

'I have a theory. If I am right, then we are all in terrible danger.'

'What do you mean?'

'We'll talk about that later. For the moment, come with me. I have something to show you.'

Eoin locks his office door from the inside then shifts one of the filing cabinets away from the wall and pushes his hand against one of the wooden panels. There is a clicking sound and the panel shifts slightly, revealing the faint outline of a door. He pushes it open and a rush of cold, musty air sweeps into the office. Will can see a dark and narrow stairwell with a lantern on the top step.

'Beaulieu is a honeycomb full of secret passages and tunnels,' says Eoin, lighting the candle in the lantern.

'But what are they for?'

'In days gone by they provided an easy escape from the enemy. Nowadays they are useful for getting to class ahead of the students. Only certain teachers know of these passages. Let's keep it that way.'

'Yes, of course.'

Will follows Eoin down and across a series of linked stairs and passages all of which are narrow and tall. Straggly cobwebs hang everywhere like deadman's bunting, wafting against his face and hair. Here and there he hears the sound of muffled voices and laughter as they pass dormitories and classrooms. The deeper they go, the colder it becomes. The air is damp all around them and the walls are dripping with moisture.

When it seems they can go down no further, Eoin stops and points to the end of the passage. 'There,' he says.

As they draw near, Will can make out a heavy, wooden cell door reinforced with steel bands. There is a small barred window. He steps closer and peers inside. The cell seems empty except for an old table.

Eoin reaches into his pocket, takes out a large key and unlocks the door. He hesitates and stares into the cell, his face gaunt and troubled. He steps inside and places the lantern on the table. Will follows him.

In a far corner, Eoin pulls a flagstone up from the floor. Underneath is a shallow hole. From it he lifts an old wooden box and sets it on the table. It looks like something a cobbler might house his tools in.

But then the box begins to tremble and the table begins to shake. Will hears a humming sound and notices flickering movements as insects begin crawling out from the cell walls seeking a way out.

'What's going on?' says Will.

Eoin cautiously opens the lid.

An unearthly blue light erupts from inside and floods the cell and the corridor beyond. Will raises his hand to shield the glare. When his eyes adjust he sees a glowing shard of blue stone, about two inches long, inside the box.

'It knows we are here. It can feel our presence, our energy, our emotions.'

'What is it?'

Eoin lifts the stone from the box and holds it up, between his thumb and index finger. 'It's a fragment.'

Tiny lights like miniature fireworks begin sparkling around Eoin's fingers and hand. Will notices his face is beginning to shine with a layer of sweat.

'A fragment of what?'

'A fragment of the Stones of Fire.'

A memory stirs in Will's mind, the muscles around his spine tighten in a snag of knots. The notebook and the Stones of Fire. They are related. But how? And then he remembers something. Something he has known. The notebook is the key to finding the Stones.

'Please hold these and go and stand the other side of the doorway,' says Eoin passing the box and the lantern from the table. Will does as he is told.

Then Eoin sets the fragment on the table and takes out a pistol from a shoulder holster under his jacket. He holds the gun by the barrel and slams the butt of the pistol down onto the fragment.

A booming sound envelops them, so loud that the walls shake. The fragment sparks furiously and streaks of blue lightning snake up and across the cell.

Eoin runs outside and closes the door. They both peer through the small window. Will watches the fragment shake angrily. The lightning sparks and surrounds the table and dry smoke fills his nostrils as the blue flames begin to consume it. In seconds the table is reduced to ash. The fragment lies among the remains, its unearthly blue light dulling to a low throb until it stops and goes out.

Will swallows. He thinks about the dream he had with a thousands voices calling out in terror. His mind swims. *Many must die for the world to change.* Where had he heard this?

'If that is what can happen with a fragment, then what are the Stones capable of?' asks Will.

'The Stones are a weapon capable of causing mass destruction. If VIPER find them, the world will be in a lot of trouble.'

'They won't find them.'

'What makes you so sure?'

'The notebook is the key to finding them. They don't not have it. We do.'

'You are correct.' Eoin re-enters the cell, places the fragment back in the box, which he places back in the hole. He slides the flagstone on top, then covers the area with dust and ash. Locking the cell, he takes the lantern and leads Will back via a different route.

'The fragment belonged to Tim Chittlock. Tim was a good friend of mine. He was a clever man, considered a crackpot by many in the service. He was a scientist, but he also believed in mysticism and magic. The Stones of Fire was a pet project of his. He was certain they were hidden somewhere in this country. But he became convinced he was being watched and followed. In our job, paranoia comes with the territory, but Tim believed he was on to something. Something bigger than all of us. Something more dangerous.'

'The Stones of Fire?'

'Yes. I didn't believe him at first – until he showed me what the fragment could do. I was shocked, but still I did not believe that the Stones would present any danger, if they could be found. He told me about the Fellowship of Fire, a secret society who guard the Stones. I thought it was more nonsense, but when the agents of VIPER started snooping around, I knew something was wrong.'

They stop at the end of a passageway, blocked by a bricked-up wall, where the acrid smell of soot claws at Will's nostrils and throat.

Eoin continues, 'Tim hid the fragment in the cell and disappeared for days. We were used to him doing this because he was often hidden away researching. Then one day he called me. He sounded erratic and hysterical and I did not know what to make of it. He said they had found him and he was in terrible danger. He was frantic. I had never heard him talk like that. I rushed to his home and found him. He had been tortured and was barely alive. I knew it was VIPER – I recognised their handiwork. He held on to me and told me he had given his notebook to the Fellowship for protection. VIPER had forced this information out of him. And then he said, "Help him…" "Who?" I asked. "Among them is a sleeper… Help him." He died moments later without saying any more.'

'I'm sorry your friend died.'

'I'm sorry too,' says Eoin. 'Tim had a man working within VIPER. He is our only hope. I believe only he can crack the codes in the notebook and find the Stones.'

Will's mouth dries. 'Do you know who he is?'

Eoin ignores the question and takes something from his pocket. It is wrapped in pale linen. He unfolds the material and reveals the notebook. 'I'm leaving for London immediately. I'd like you to take this and look after it.'

Will takes the notebook and stares at it, relieved to have it in his hands again yet overwhelmed at the secrets it contains. The thought of the Stones and the damage they can cause terrifies him. He wonders about the Fellowship and how they fit in this expanding spider's web. Timothy Chittlock clearly trusted them. But why?

How could anyone trust an organisation with someone like the Pastor as a member?

Eoin turns towards the wall, pulls out a loose brick and peers through to the other side. He pulls a metal catch above his shoulder and the wall turns inwards. Will is surprised to see the Great Hall on the other side. They are in the fireplace.

'Whoever killed Tim did not get what they wanted. I told you Tim was clever. He was always one step ahead of us, and them. Somehow he managed to plant a spy in the Agents of VIPER camp; a double agent training to be one of them and learning all their secrets. This person patiently and calmly waited to carry out his mission. People like this are known as sleepers. Tim's double agent would be an unknown, someone outside the norm. Someone whom no one would suspect. Who better than a young man such as yourself?'

Will feels his muscles coil. 'What do you mean?'

'I think that person is you, Will. I think that you are Tim's sleeper.'

Chapter 20

The Siege

That evening Will is lying on top of his bunk, basking in the warm yellow glow from his bedside lamp. His mind is racing. Eoin's theory that he is a sleeper agent turns over and over in his mind. It seems preposterous, but it would explain his fighting and shooting abilities. These are not the skills of an average sixteen-year-old. But why would his parents let him be an agent – and a sleeper agent of all things? People are trying to kill him. Wouldn't those dangers have crossed his parents' minds? What sort of parents would let their children do that sort of thing? He feels an ache for the family he does not remember and shifts uneasily in his bunk. He wonders if this ache is because he does not remember them or, worse, because they are dead. He hugs his arms and tries to think about something else.

He hears Edward stirring in his bunk at the other side of the room. He thinks he may be waking. He could do with someone to talk to right now, even if it is Edward, but seconds later his roommate snores quietly.

Will sighs and thinks about the fragment, the Stones of Fire and their disturbing ethereal power. He is still not entirely sure what to make of it all. But seeing what the fragment is capable of has made him think there is more in this world than he thought possible. It is exciting and terrifying. Because of the notebook there have been three deaths already and, if Eoin is right, and VIPER get the notebook and Stones, there will be many more deaths too. He looks at the notebook resting on the bedside table. The location of the Stones is hidden somewhere in the coded text. For a moment he thinks he should destroy the book, burn it to ash so that no one will ever find the Stones. But what if someone already knows where they are? What if they find the Stones and sell them to VIPER? His gut twists at the thought and then something clicks inside him and he realises what he must do.

He spends the next few hours poring over the text, trying to decipher the codes. He scrawls on sheets of paper and places the sheets on the floor, rearranging them into some sort of order.

Wrapped up in the job at hand, he does not hear Edward rising, nor does he realise his roommate is standing behind him studying the sheets of paper and trying to unravel the mystery code.

'Move the top sheet two to the right and then move sheet four to the bottom and then…' says Edward.

Will jumps and spins round, 'What are you doing?' he snaps.

Edward jolts. 'I… I was just trying to help.'

Will stares at him for a moment and then looks back at the papers. This was taking him a long time and he didn't seem to be getting very far. What harm would it do to have a second pair of eyes?

'I'm sorry, Edward. I didn't mean to shout. I could really do with some help.'

Edward beams, crouches down, and begins rearranging the sheets.

'Look at the code. It has a rhythm. Do you see it?'

Will studies the lines and begins to see a repetition of some symbols. But that is all he can see.

'It could be a prayer,' says Edward, tapping his head. 'Or a poem.'

Edward smiles.

'What is it?'

'It's a song.'

'A what?'

'A song.'

Will frowns, not quite believing him. Edward begins writing on one of the sheets while humming a tune. Will recognises it immediately.

Oranges and lemons,
Say the bells of St Clement's.
You owe me five farthings,
Say the bells of St Martin's.
When will you pay me?
Say the bells of Old Bailey.
When I grow rich,
Say the bells of Shoreditch.
When will that be?
Say the bells of Stepney.
I do not know,
Says the great bell of Bow.

Will stares at the words on the sheet. It is the tune from his dream only two nights back. Of course. That is it. He rubs the back of his neck, trying to imagine what its relevance could be.

There is a knock on the door. Will opens it. Violet is standing in the doorway. 'Hello handsome,' she says.

'Erm... hello.'

'There's a telephone call for you in the Major's office.'

Will's eyes flash. It could be Eoin. He glances back at Edward. 'Keep at it. I'll be back soon.'

At the Major's office he stops outside and knocks twice.

'Come,' she calls.

The Major is sitting at her desk and talking into the phone. 'Yes... yes... of course,' she says, her face grey and solemn. She looks up at Will. 'He's here now, Eoin. Would you like to speak to him?' She hands the phone to Will.

'Hello...' says Will.

But there is no answer.

'Eoin… It's me.' Silence. And then Will can hear voices shouting, followed by gunfire. His grip on the phone tightens. 'Eoin! Eoin! Can you hear me?' he shouts.

Eoin does not respond. There is more gunfire and, in the distance, a great bell chimes. Will has heard it many times before. It is Big Ben.

Will glances at the Major. Her face has clouded over.

'What did he say?' says Will, his stomach a storm of knots.

'He has discovered more about your past and believes the school, and you especially, are in great danger. He says we have to get *it* out of here immediately. They are coming. They might even be here already.'

'Who are *they?*'

'That remains to be seen. Eoin requested I take you away from here immediately.' The Major opens one of the drawers in her desk, takes out a revolver and starts filling it with bullets. 'Do not worry about Eoin, Mr Starling. He is a remarkable man. Now, would you like to explain to me what this is all about?'

But Will is only half listening. Through the window he can see shadows moving quickly across the school grounds. He feels the hairs on his neck rising. Something is not right. And then he hears the sound of glass breaking from the direction of the Great Hall. It is followed by several gunshots. Someone screams.

The Major's eyes widen. 'Good Lord, he was right. They are here!'

Will feels himself go cold. He has left the notebook unprotected with Edward. He runs to the door and pulls it open.

'Will, wait!' calls the Major, but he is already out of the office and sprinting towards the Great Hall.

Smoke is beginning to fill the area. Several gunshots ring out and he hears more screaming and shouting. He can see several canisters strewn across the floor with smoke billowing furiously from them. He pulls a handkerchief from his pocket and covers his mouth and nose. He hears voices and looks in their direction. Through the haze, he sees Anna and Violet fighting a man with a gas mask covering his face. In one hand he holds a torch, in the other, a pistol. The smoke is getting the better of Anna and Violet. Will can see they are weakening. A shot rings out. Violet stumbles into the smoke and Anna falls to her knees coughing. The man in the mask looms over her, his pistol pointing at her head.

A surge of anger grips Will. He charges forward, stiffening his muscles in preparation for maximum impact. The man does not see him coming. Will hits him full pelt in the ribs. The gunman grunts as the air expels from his lungs as if from a burst tyre. He topples back, dropping the torch. Will falls to his knees and gasps. Violet is lying on the floor with a bloody chest, her lifeless eyes stare blankly into the smoke. He scrambles back and collides with someone.

'Violet. Is that you?' says Anna.

Will's heart pounds in his chest.

The gunfire starts again from all sides of the Great Hall. Picking up the discarded torch, and stuffing it in his pocket, Will ducks and grabs Anna's hand. 'Come with me!' he says, pulling her across the smoke-filled room. She resists.

'Anna, it's me, Will!'

'Violet!' she calls, ignoring him.

Will has lost the handkerchief in the charge and covers his mouth and nose with his arm, his eyes stinging and streaming. Bullets fly past their ears.

'We have to go!' shouts Will, and hauls her to a halt beside the fireplace. He hears the voices of other students arriving in the hall and hopes they are armed. Groping the wall above the chimney breast, he searches for the unlocking mechanism. He pushes and fumbles blindly for what seems like an age until eventually something clicks. The wall inside the fireplace opens.

They stumble through. Will presses the closing mechanism. The wall starts to close agonisingly slowly. As it does, Will sees emerging through the smoke a figure carrying a sniper's rifle. It is not a masked man but a pupil.

Horne.

'Get out of here, Horne!' cries Will, coughing.

Horne looks around him searching to pinpoint the location of Will's voice.

'Run, Horne!'

Horne raises the rifle and swings it across the room.

The wall slides shut. Will hears the sound of rapid gunfire and wonders if Horne has killed someone, or has been killed himself. But something niggles at him. Why was Horne not shooting at the masked men? Did he hate Will so much that he was taking the chance to hunt for him?

Will and Anna stand for a moment coughing and wiping their eyes, listening to the gunfire on the other side of the wall.

'What's happening?' says Anna.

'The school is under attack.'

'From whom?'

'I don't know,' says Will, though he has no doubt VIPER are behind it.

'How did you know about this place?'

'It's a long story.'

'I have to go back out. Violet is still out there.'

'Anna, we have to leave.'

'Not without Violet!'

'We can't go back out there.'

'Open the door!'

'It's too late!'

'What are you talking about?'

'We should just go.'

'Not without Violet!'

'She's dead, Anna!'

There is a stillness in the air between them; the only sounds are the muffled blasts from the other side of the fireplace.

'She… she can't be. We were just… You're lying!'

'I'm sorry, Anna. I wish I was. But you must trust me. If you want to live, then come with me.'

Anna says nothing for a moment.

'Who did this?'

'I think it is VIPER. Please, come with me.'

Anna says nothing.

'Fine! Stay here then.' Will points the torchlight down the passage and glances at Anna. In the briefest of seconds he sees the grief on Anna's face transform to a cold determination.

'We should hurry,' he says.

Thankfully, Anna allows him to lead her away through the underground tunnel. He tries to get his bearings and takes them up a stairwell that he hopes runs up the west turret. Through the walls, he can hear more gunfire and explosions and feels sick with guilt that he is not helping.

He stops at the top of the stairs, places his ear against the wall and listens. There is nothing. He shines the beam on the unlocking mechanism and pushes it. There is a creaking sound and a portion of the wall opens. He peers cautiously up and down. They are in the boys' bathroom. The light is bright and it smells of stale, damp towels.

They climb through the opening and run down to Will and Edward's room. He stops at the bedroom door and listens. There is silence. He peeks inside. Edward is huddled in the corner, trembling, his face pale. Will looks around him. There is no one else there. He breathes a sigh of relief and grabs the papers, stuffing them into the fireplace and lighting them with a match. He takes off the Beaulieu blazer, puts on his old one and slips the notebook into his side pocket. Looking at Edward he says. 'We have to get out of here.'

But Edward shakes his head. Will walks toward him and speaks calmly. 'If you stay here, you will almost certainly die.'

The sound of gunfire is drawing closer but still Edward does not budge.

'Edward, come with me. I will keep you safe, I promise,' says Will, even though he knows it is a promise he may not be able to keep.

Anna takes Edward's hand. 'It'll be fine, Eddie. Just come with us.'

Edward trembles and then nods his head slowly.

Will glances out of the bedroom door. Smoke is rising from the west turret stairs. Their only choice is to run in the opposite direction. They hurry up the corridor. He hears a shot and a bullet embeds itself in the stone inches from his head. He turns to see a man, broad and well-built with dark hair, his face obscured with a gas mask, emerging from the smoke. Will has seen him before. He feels his mouth drying. It is Colonel Victor Frost.

Chapter 21

Exploding Rats

Frost points his gun at Will but the billowing smoke obscures his aim. Will wastes no time. This is their only chance.

'Run!' he shouts.

Bullets fly in their wake. Turning a corner, a window looks out over the grounds. The moon shimmers on bodies lying on the ground near the garage. He is unsure if they are students, teachers or the enemy. He catches sight of the vivid green turban of Mr Singh. He is brandishing a pistol in each hand, shooting without conscience at two masked men. Will feels a glimmer of hope as he sprints up the corridor.

They turn a second corner and his heart sinks. It is a dead end. He spins round to see Frost and two other men in masks. Frost removes his mask and stares cold and hard at Will.

'Give me the notebook, Will,' he says.

'No,' says Will. 'Never.'

Frost smiles calmly. 'Kill them,' he says to his companions. The two men raise their guns. Will steps in front of Anna and Edward, shielding them. He has to think fast. 'Wait. I'll give you what you want. You don't need to hurt them.'

'How good of you to give me an option.'

Will feels a draught and hears a ticking sound from the floor. Two small clockwork rats scuttle from either side of his legs towards the three men. They are the low-impact explosives type. Enough for a diversion. He throws himself back as they explode, narrowly missing a volley of gunfire.

'Will, this way,' says a voice to his left. He turns to see a narrow opening in the wall that Anna and Edward have already entered. Eli is standing just inside. Will leaps into the passageway and slams the door shut behind him.

He hears Frost's guttural voice. 'You cannot escape me, Will. Not now. Not ever.'

Will feels his blood run cold.

Eli is holding a lantern. It lights the dark space with a dim, shadowy light.

'You need to get far away from here,' he says. 'Take Miss Wilder and Edward, too. Go to the garage – a driver is waiting for you in Eoin's Embiricos. There is a radio in the boot. It is charged and ready. Once you're safe, send out the distress call, "*The birds have flown the nest*". Let us know where you are and we will find you. Got that?'

'Yes. But what about you?'

'Never mind me. I can look after meself.'

Eli pulls some coins from his pocket and hands them across.

Will frowns.

'Just in case. There should be enough here to tide you over for a day or two.'

There is a battering sound from the corridor outside.

Will takes the coins.

'I will hold off our friends. Follow the stairs all the way down. Mr Singh will cover you.'

Will removes the torch from his pocket and switches it on. 'Good luck, Eli.'

The old poacher smiles. 'You might find something useful in the back of my old van, if you have time to look.'

'Thank you.' But Will is not sure what he means by this.

'Mind how you go, now.'

As the pounding increases, Will hurries down the stairs with Edward and Anna behind him. Around them, on the other side of the walls, he can hear the sound of shouting and gunfire. He hears the Major barking orders and then a rally of gunshots. He hopes they all come out of this alive. Then, suddenly, they reach a stone wall at the bottom of the passageway stairs; it seems they can go no further. He shines the torchlight over the wall, searching for the unlocking mechanism. But it is just stones and nothing else. He starts pushing them randomly and is joined by Anna and Edward who follow his lead. At last something clicks. The wall opens under their collective weight and they fall out into the path of an armed man wearing a mask. Edward stands up and backs away. The man raises his gun.

'No!' cries Edward, and then a shot drowns out his voice.

Will's heart pounds.

'Edward!' he calls, but Edward is still standing. The masked man falls to his knees and crumples forward on to the ground. Behind him, Will sees Mr Singh approaching with his guns pointing at the man. Mr Singh kicks the body, confirming he is dead and then looks towards to the garage where the Embiricos and the old Post Office van are parked.

'The driver is dead,' he says.

Will sees the bloodied body of the driver at the entrance to the garage. In his hand are the car keys. Will glances at the Embiricos and back at the keys. He has no memory of learning to drive, yet he knows that somewhere in his hidden past he has been behind the wheel of a car.

'I can drive,' he says.

Mr Singh looks at him, his brow furrowed. Then he nods. 'Go. I will cover you.'

Will turns to Edward and Anna: 'Wait here both of you!'

'Where are you going?' says Anna, but Will scans the area for any signs of hidden gunmen. There seems to be none, but it is dark and they could be hiding.

'Ready?' says Mr Singh

'Ready,' says Will, running furiously toward the garage. Bullets pelt the gravel in his wake as he snatches the keys from the dead man's hand, dives inside and rolls across the floor between the Embiricos and Eli's van. Panting, he lies low for a second. He crawls to the rear of Eli's van, curious about what he meant by *something useful*. Inside are a stack of rat bombs. He grabs four of them and tosses them into the Embiricos.

When he jumps into the driver's seat he feels an immediate familiarity with the wheel and controls. Relieved he starts up the engine. It rumbles into life like a growling lion. Slipping it into gear, he accelerates and speeds out of the garage, swerving in the gravel to stop beside Anna and Edward. Bullets prang off the bodywork, much to his relief. They might just get out of here alive. He leans across and pushes open the passenger door: 'Get in!' he shouts.

They clamber inside. Edward squeezes himself into the back and lies down for cover. 'There's rats in here!' he cries.

'Go, now, quickly!' Mr Singh shouts. Will glances in the side mirror and sees him face off three gunmen who are running towards them.

Anna pulls the door closed and Will slams the accelerator and speeds away from the house and on into the night.

He throttles the Embiricos through the dark country lanes, his hands gripping the steering wheel, his concentration firmly on the road ahead. He is not sure where they are going but he knows he has to get far away from Beaulieu. His pulse is racing, blood pounds in his ears, drowning out the barrage of questions from Anna and Edward.

He knows Frost's cars will follow them soon enough. They must keep going, but to where? Think. Think. Of course! There is only one place. He glances at the petrol gauge, sees it is almost empty and swears under his breath.

'What's the time?'

'Will, tell me what is going on?' demands Anna.

'Who were those people?' Edward stutters.

'The time... what time is it now?' says Will, raising his voice, his patience thinning fast.

There is a pause and Edward speaks, 'Forty minutes past nine.'

Will nods. 'We have time.'

'For what?' says Anna.

The road widens, clear in the light of the half moon. Will spins the wheel, tossing his passengers to the side as the Embiricos skids and faces the direction they have just come. In the distance, he can see the outline of Beaulieu. The west turret is on fire and smoke is billowing from other parts of the house.

They say nothing for a moment. Then Edward breaks the silence. Do you think they are all dead?

'I hope not,' says Will. 'But we can't worry about that now.' Part of him regrets not staying to fight but he knows it was too dangerous. The notebook would be in the hands of the enemy and he, Anna and Edward would also be dead.

He sees the beams of three cars leaving Beaulieu and driving quickly in the direction he had driven. He takes three deep breaths and rolls the car forward into the shadows of a small copse. He switches off the growling engine.

'Get down, you two,' he says, and slides down the seat himself.

With hooded eyes, peeking over the dashboard, Will watches three Austin 8s fly past. He breathes a sigh of relief but freezes as he hears the screech of brakes. From the side mirror he sees the rear lights of the last car as it stops dead in the middle of the road. He holds his breath and waits. The door opens and a man gets out and peers in their direction through a pair of binoculars.

They have been spotted.

Will closes his eyes in an effort to think. What can he do? And then he remembers. 'Edward, pass me two rats.'

Edward hands them across and Will turns the clockwork keys just as the man jumps back into his car.

He starts up the Embiricos and drives out of the copse. Opening the driver's door, he places the rats on the ground, their wheels carrying them obediently toward the car that is now reversing towards them.

Will pushes his foot down on the accelerator and, through the rear-view mirror, watches with a measure of satisfaction as the rats explode under the car, causing it to swerve off the road. The three men escape, shaken, and stumble onto the road, coughing.

'Where are we going?' asks Anna.

'We're going to catch a train.'

Chapter 22

The 9.59 to London

Will knows that the Embiricos' beautiful styling and fearsome engine will not allow them to disappear quietly and unseen. He drives cautiously towards the station and parks off the road in a concealed spot, a short distance away. He is relieved they have not been followed, but knows that could all change in a moment. They have to be quick. He opens the driver's door and turns to Edward.

'Bring the other two rats. Just in case.'

Edward's face is grave but he lifts them tentatively as if they might explode at any minute.

Will opens the boot. Inside is a small suitcase containing the radio, which is much heavier than it looks. There is also a shoulder bag, made from battered brown leather. He fishes it out, pulls the strap across his shoulder and puts the rats gently into the bag. He closes the boot, locks the car doors and rests his hand on its warm bonnet, caressing it. He does not want to leave it, but they have no choice. He reaches for the radio, but Anna beats him to it.

'It's heavy,' says Will.

Anna's right eyebrow arches. 'You think because I am a girl, I can't carry a radio?'

'Erm… no,' says Will, 'That's not what I meant… Sorry.'

'Good,' she replies, tartly.

Will looks away quickly then leads Anna and Edward towards Brockenhurst Station.

'What is the plan?' says Anna

'We go to London.'

'Why London?'

'Eoin is there for a start. And the churches mentioned in "Oranges and Lemons" are there.'

'"Oranges and Lemons"?' asks Anna.

'I'll explain later. We need to hurry,' says Will, stepping into the station office. Anna follows, but Edward doesn't budge.

'We should stay here and wait for a rescue party,' says Edward.

'Edward, we had a lucky escape,' says Will. 'Those men are looking for us and will be here very soon. By the time a rescue party arrives, we will be dead.'

'You don't know that!' snaps Edward.

'I'm not prepared to risk it!'

Edward trembles in silence.

Will takes a breath, and tries to remain calm. 'We are going to London, Edward. You are not staying behind.'

Anna speaks up. 'Will's right, Eddie. We have to get out of here.'

Edward fidgets with his blazer. 'I'm not going to London and that's that.'

'They will kill you like they did the others,' says Anna.

A whistle blows. 'Last train to London,' calls the guard.

Will glances at the station clock. It is 9.59. In the near distance, he hears the sound of speeding cars approaching. 'They're coming!' He tries to grab Edward's arm but Edward pulls away and runs toward the station exit.

Anna drops the radio and runs after him but he is gone.

'There is nothing we can do, Anna,' says Will. 'We have to go.'

She rounds on him, her eyes wild and furious as if this is all his fault. He turns away and looks toward the platform. 'Stay if you want to!' he says, picking up the case, but Anna takes it from him and together they run towards the train.

'You're too late, you're too late,' the guard shouts, his arms out blocking their path, but they push past and sprint to the door of the last carriage. Will is first and pulls it open. Anna climbs up, heaving the radio with her.

Will watches as Frost and his men run onto the platform. The train rolls forward gaining speed. Steam billows down the platform and through it Will can see a furious Frost, baring his teeth and running ahead of the others, but he is not fast enough and skids to a stop as the train hurries away from Brockenhurst. Will can just make out Frost's angry face melding into the swirling steam and breathes a sigh of relief. He sits down and wonders where Edward is. He hopes he has the sense to hide long enough to survive this.

The train rumbles into the night. The carriage is quiet, with only a handful of occupants who glance suspiciously at Will and Anna, huddled together and whispering. Will is mindful and keeps an eye on them as he explains as much as he can about the notebook, the Stones of Fire, his memory loss and what has happened to him.

For a while, Anna does not say anything. She ponders what Will has just told her. Eventually, she breaks the silence. 'Do you believe the Stones can create fire?'

Will wants to tell her about the fragment, but the less everyone knows the better for now.

'No,' he says, avoiding her eyes. 'But some people do and are prepared to kill for them.'

'It's clearly some sort of silly myth,' she says. 'Essentially stone is composed of grains of minerals arranged in an orderly manner. The aggregate minerals forming the rock are held together by chemical bonds, none of which, to my knowledge, are combustible or can create fire. Unless...' She pauses.

'Unless what?'

'Unless the stone is flint. Even then, you would need a piece of steel and all that could be achieved is a spark.'

Will understands the supernatural mythology of the Stones is hard to swallow. He tries to smile at Anna's logical explanation although he is impressed with her scientific knowledge.

'At Beaulieu,' says Anna, changing the subject, 'you could shoot and fight better than any of the other students. Where did you learn to do that?'

Will shifts uneasily in his chair. 'I told you I lost my memory. I... I don't know.'

Anna watches him through narrowed eyes.

Does she think he is an enemy spy?

After a moment she shrugs. 'If the Major and Eoin trust you, then I do too.'

'Forget that for now. We need a plan for London. We are not out of the woods yet.'

'Agreed. We could just make our way to Baker Street,' she says.

'No. That is what they will expect us to do.'

'Then what do you propose?'

Will sits forward and Anna leans closer to hear what he has to say.

It is almost midnight when the train approaches Victoria. In line with blackout restrictions, all carriage lights are switched off. In the bright moonlight, the London skyline fills Will with a mixture of emotions just like it did on *The Outcast*. He feels excited as if he is somehow returning home, even though he has no memories of the city beyond waking up on *The Outcast* four days ago. But like then, he has other things to think about now, other concerns lie ahead. All that matters now is finding the Stones before VIPER do.

The other passengers begin to gather their belongings and make their way to the aisle outside the carriage as they prepare for the train to stop.

Will and Anna stand by the doors that face away from the platform. As the train slows Will pushes open the door. 'Good luck,' he says to Anna.

'Thanks.'

She steps to the open door and jumps, landing with the grace of a cat on the walkway between the tracks. She springs up immediately and runs alongside the train, her arms open. Will tosses the suitcase in her direction. She catches it, but it slides from her grip and falls on to the track opposite. Will's heart sinks.

'Please don't be broken,' he whispers in a quiet prayer.

The train comes to a stop and Will follows the other passengers onto the platform, mingling among them as if he was a member of one of the families. He scans the platform for anyone suspicious but it is dark, which is in his favour.

He spots four male silhouettes at the entrance to the concourse. One of them greets a passenger with a handshake and another opens his arms to a woman who runs enthusiastically toward him.

The other two men remain watchful. With his head down, Will walks with the other passengers, quickening his pace as he see one of the men pointing in his direction. Both men turn and start navigating the crowd as if tailing him.

Will dashes ahead and, with relief, sees Anna hurry out of sight and onto Victoria Street. Cheered by the knowledge that their plan to split up is so far successful, he turns and runs across the main concourse.

He steers a course away from Anna, through a corridor, which is thankfully empty. Will sprints down it, winding up a rat bomb at the same time. He hears the echoing footfalls of the men behind him, stops and turns to face them, his heart pounding in his chest.

'Do you know what this is?' he shouts, waving the rat. The men slow and do not respond, but he knows they are wary. 'Don't think I won't use it.'

One of them laughs and reaches into his pocket, but Will tosses the rat and runs. There is a gunshot and he ducks as a bullet chips the wall to his left. The rat explodes and a cloud of dust and masonry follows him out of the tunnel and onto the street outside. Wilton Street. He coughs and runs towards Victoria Street where he hears Anna's voice. She is sitting in the back of a black cab. He jumps inside.

The driver, a bulldog of a man, stares at the smoky corridor. 'Was that a bomb?' he says.

'I think so,' says Will, coughing, his mouth dry with the smoke and dust.

'You was lucky, mate. Blimey, we get no peace here. Where to?'

Will has not thought about that. Where could they go? They need somewhere that is close and remote enough to use the radio without attracting attention. He thinks hard and recalls a place hidden deep in the folds of his memory. 'Primrose Hill, please.'

'Primrose Hill, it is,' says the driver.

Will glances back at the corridor. There is no sign of the men. He is relieved, but also terrified. Had he just killed them?

Chapter 23

Primrose Hill

The cab driver drives up Regents Park Road and pulls over. Will hands across some of Eli's coins, gets out and waits until the cab is out of sight.

'How do you know this place?' asks Anna.

Will hesitates before answering. 'I don't remember how – I just do,' he says, recalling Skipper's story of the friend who had lost his memory. The poor man had not recognised family or friends yet he knew the town where he had lived all his life. He had gone mad in the end. Will shudders.

'Why here?' asks Anna.

'The hill will provide us a clear, open space where we can operate the radio without interruption. We should be safe here for the time being. Once we get a signal out, they'll come and get us.'

They trek across the darkness and settle on a secluded spot at the top of the hill under the protection of some bushes. Will sits on the damp grass, takes out the torch, and shines its beam at the suitcase. The radio is neatly built inside. Just like the one at Beaulieu, it has a large rectangular power pack and a panel with dials and buttons, which operate the transmitter and the receiver. There is a compartment that holds the headphones and strapped inside the suitcase lid is the user manual.

He puts on the headphones and switches on the radio. Turning the dial, he listens for a signal, but there is nothing.

'I think it's broken.'

'I'm sorry I dropped it.'

'It was my stupid idea to throw it off the train. I should have taken it with me.'

'It wasn't stupid. You would never have got away from those men if you were carrying it.'

She edges closer and Will can feel the heat from her body. It feels strange having her so close, this girl who was so dismissive of him, but he likes it.

Focusing on the radio, he removes the headphones, reaches for the manual and starts paging through it for clues. There is a diagram of the chassis, which he recognises from Radio Operations class. He wonders about Mr Singh and the selfless way he had saved them and hopes he has survived the siege.

He unclips the transceiver panel, places it on the grass and shines the beam into the chassis. The power connector is in place and the fuses are all seated. The scale lamps are intact and the earthing leads are in place. So what is the problem? He leans forward for a closer look and peers in through the gap that houses the power connections.

There is a loose wire.

'Got it,' he says, his fingers reaching through the gap. The solder holding the power supply wires to the chassis is broken. He spots an excess of wire on another connection, turns to Anna and hands her the torch. 'Would you mind?'

She smiles and points the beam at the chassis. Will is thankful he had the sense to put on his old blazer. He removes the wire cutters from the sleeve of his blazer, cuts the wire and wraps it round the broken solder, reconnecting the power supply.

'Fingers crossed, that will do it,' he says.

He switches the radio on, but there is still no response. He turns dials and knobs and pushes the On/Off button several times. He looks at Anna who regards him quizzically.

'Maybe the power supply is flat,' she offers.

Will isn't so sure. Eli had told him it was charged. He recalls a trick Mr

Singh had shown him when the school's transistor radio was unresponsive. He lifts his hand and slaps the side of the radio. It trembles and sparks into life.

Will and Anna smile at each other as he turns the tuning dial. The sound of white noise and static crackles through the headphones. Relief sweeps over him.

'Well done, Will.'

'How is your Morse code?'

'As good as anyone's,' she says, and confidently reaches for the radio. She looks at Will, 'The birds have flown the nest?'

'That's what Eli said.'

Will watches transfixed as Anna puts on the headphones and starts pressing the telegraph key. After a moment he closes his eyes and takes three deep breaths. At last they might get out of this mess.

Almost two hours pass with no luck. They huddle together to keep warm as Anna continues tapping the distress call at intervals, her free hand poised with a pencil and paper, ready to write down instructions.

Will is concerned the battery may not last much longer and is about to think of a back-up plan when Anna looks up.

'They've heard us.'

'At last! What do they say?'

There is a pause and then Anna begins scribbling on the paper.

..... . / ... .- ..-. . / .... --- .. .- ... . / .---- ...--.. / .- -... -... . . .-. .-.. .. -. . / ... - .-... - / .-- .... .. - . -.-. .... .- .--...-..

None of it means anything to Will. 'What does it say?'

'The safe house 13 Abberline Street Whitechapel. Do you know Whitechapel?'

Will shakes his head. 'No, but I will get us there somehow. We should wait until morning. Those men, if they are still alive, may be looking for us. There may be others too. At least during the day we can blend in with the crowds.'

* * *

Anna lies down to try and get some rest. Will does not intend to sleep and he does not want to worry Anna. As the hours pass, his fertile imagination makes him think VIPER had seen him get into the taxi, tracked down the driver, who told them Will and Anna were sitting all alone on top of Primrose Hill. They could be on their way here right now. He shakes his head and pushes the thought from his head.

He looks at the text in the notebook under the torchlight, hoping to unravel some clues.

'Do you really think the Stones are in London?' says Anna.

'I think so.'

'You don't seem very sure.'

'I could be wrong, but it just seems the right place to start, considering Edward's translation of "Oranges and Lemons".' Will pockets the notebook and switches off the torch. He can feel Anna appraising him. Perhaps she thinks he is mad.

'We should get some rest. It will be dawn soon. I'll keep watch,' he says, rubbing his hands to keep them warm.

As he sits in the silence before dawn, the gravity of their situation plays on his mind. The siege of Beaulieu was horrific. His stomach clenches at the image of Violet lying dead in the Great Hall. And what of Edward, Eli, the Major, Mr Singh and the others? Were they dead? He does not want to contemplate that. This was all because of the notebook and the Stones. The responsibility for finding them is now down to him. Wasn't it always? he thinks, hugging his knees tight to his chest. And what has happened to Eoin? He might be the only person to have uncovered information about Will's past. Was he dead too? Was he gone forever and, with him, the keys to Will's memories that he so wanted back?

'Are you alright?' whispers Anna, interrupting his thoughts.

Will looks in her direction. She is sitting up and looking back at him with a concerned expression.

'I'm fine,' he lies, but the truth is, he is terrified. He is a stranger in his own body, caught up in a quest to find a terrible weapon in the middle of a world at war. How did this ever happen? He wants to pour it all out to her, but the sound of bird song shows that dawn has snuck on up them. The first rays of the sun dapple through the gaps in the bushes and lifts his spirit. They still have a chance to get through this, but first they have to find the safe house. Will does not know Whitechapel and finding Abberline Street might be tricky.

'We should go,' he says.

Anna nods in agreement.

Will heaves up his cold and stiff limbs, straightens his tie, and combs his hair into a side parting with his fingers.

'Best we don't look as if we have been sleeping in the bushes all night.'

Anna begins to brush off the grass and twigs from his clothes. She takes a comb from her pocket and sweeps it through Will's hair. She fixes his tie properly.

'That's better,' she says, stepping back and combing her own shiny brown hair.

Will feels a little flush inside and smiles.

Anna smiles back and pockets her comb.

Together they walk out of the bushes and into the open space of Primrose Hill where, through the whitebeam trees, they can see the city of London waking up and beginning a new day.

Will looks east, in the direction of Whitechapel, which is a long walk from where they are standing. 'We should go. We can take turns carrying the radio,' he says.

They leave Primrose Hill and walk onto Regents Park Road. It is still very early and the only signs of life are the blackout blinds being drawn from the windows of early risers.

They walk to Camden Town and into the tube station where early commuters are beginning their journeys to work. With the last of their money they buy two single tickets to Whitechapel.

The train pulls into the platform and Will sees their reflection in the carriage windows. His picture has been in the newspapers and the Beaulieu crest on Anna's breast pocket is an unusual feature. They both stand out.

'We need a change of clothes,' he says.

The train stops, the guard alights, and cranks open the doors.

'They keep all sorts of supplies, including clothes, in safe houses,' says Anna.

'Good,' says Will, relieved there will be one less thing to worry about.

The guard blows his whistle and hops quickly onto the train, cranking the doors shut as Will and Anna huddle among the throng.

'We have no clue where Abberline Street is. If only we had a map.'

'Leave that to me,' says Anna, who turns and threads her way through the commuters.

Will watches as she talks to the guard, her face warm and smiling, a different person from the one she usually reveals.

'What did you say to him?'

'I asked him where the nearest library was. We can get a map there.'

Chapter 24

The Safe House

Friday, 9th May 1941

The guard has directed them to Bishopsgate Library. Will thinks the library an odd building, resembling a narrow castle, sandwiched in between two equally narrow but much less grand blocks of flats.

A thin balding librarian nods curtly to them as they enter. His eyes linger on the crest of Anna's blazer. Does he recognise the criss-crossed pistols and dagger? Will feels a fluttering sensation in his stomach and considers leaving, but the librarian looks away casually and starts putting books onto the shelves. Will relaxes and decides that he is just being paranoid.

No one else gives them a second glance as they make their way to the shelves of maps. They could be students visiting the library for a day of study, or so Will hopes.

The reference area is quiet and warm with the familiar and welcoming smell of dry and dusty books. Will wastes no time and quickly finds the *London A-to-Z*. Anna keeps a lookout, ensuring no one is watching, and shields him as he shoves it into the bag.

'Got it?' she says.

'Yes.'

Will sees a sign for Ancient History books and has an idea.

'Let's go,' says Anna.

'Not yet.'

A man's voice interrupts their exchange. 'May I help you young people.'

The librarian is standing beside them. Up close, Will takes stock of him. He is dressed in a brown tweed suit and wears a garish yellow bow tie.

'We're looking for Greek mythology.'

The Librarian narrows his gaze at Will and points to their left.

'Thank you,' says Will, looking away, hoping the man's prolonged look was not down to recognising him from the newspapers.

He starts to scan the bookshelf labelled Mythology unsure what he is hoping to find.

He hears someone approach and feels his muscles tensing.

'Have you travelled far?' asks the librarian.

'Yes. We're from St Luke's,' says Anna, quick off the mark.

'St Luke's? I can't say I've heard of it.'

'It's in Wimbledon,' she says.

'Yes, Wimbledon,' says Will.

'Oh, well, I don't know that area very well.'

'Where can I find books on the Restoration?' says Anna, changing the subject.

The librarian hesitates before answering. 'This way, if you please. The subject is a speciality of mine, actually.'

'Oh, that's nice.'

Will listens to their voices fade and then starts pulling books on Greek mythology from the shelves. He leafs through them, scanning their contents for clues. Ten minutes pass, then twenty, but he finds nothing of value. From the other side of the library, he feels Anna staring at him and he looks up.

'We should go,' she mouths.

She is right of course. They are wasting valuable time and besides, he is unsettled by the librarian, who is still hovering around. Will nods and starts putting the books back. He sees one shelf labelled Greek Gods. Suddenly he feels dizzy; something begins to unravel in his head and he tries to push through the folds of his mind.

Think… think… come on! Something dating back years – something from biblical times and something long before that.

Confusion clouds his thoughts and he steadies himself against the shelf. His fingers brush against a book called *Greeks Gods and the Thracians*. Something sparks inside of him. That's it! He makes sure no one is watching and slips the book inside the bag next to the *A to Z*.

He finds Anna, pretending to browse the shelves. He catches her eye and nods. They leave quickly and hurry up Bishopsgate Road, with their heads down.

'Something came to me in the library. A memory of something I once knew, but it was patchy with little to hook on to. I think it is something to do with the Stones being inlaid in Moses' Breastplate of Judgement. And there was also suggestion the Stones could be of Greek origin. I found a book that might hold some answers.'

Using the *A to Z*, Will and Anna find their way to Abberline Street, a dingy little road tucked away in the dark recesses of Whitechapel, where it seems the sun rarely, if ever, shines. Damp and slippery cobbles make for slow and difficult progress. The houses are rundown Victorian tenements from which come the sound of mothers at the end of their tether, and babies crying for attention and food. A skinny boy with a dirty face and grave expression watches them approach. He reminds Will of Sam. Will smiles to himself and wonders where Sam is.

'Number thirteen,' says Anna, pointing.

It is dark inside, but Will could swear he caught sight of movement.

'Someone is inside.'

'Yes, I saw.'

'We should let them know we are here,' he says, stepping forward and knocking the door. From the other side, he hears the sound of footsteps on a wooden floor, the clicking turn of the lock and the sliding of a heavy bolt. The door swings open and a stout woman in a headscarf and housecoat stands in the doorway: ''allo dears,' she says. 'I've been expecting you.'

She glances quickly up and down the street and then beckons them inside. 'In you pop.'

Will follows Anna into a dimly lit hallway, their feet echoing on the bare floorboards. He notices there is no ornamentation or decoration inside that might reveal it as the entrance hall to someone's home. If anything it feels empty and cold.

The woman locks and bolts the door. 'You took your time,' she says.

'Who are you?' asks Will.

'You can call me Aunty. Everyone does.' She smiles at them with crooked and chipped teeth.

The smell of something savoury drifts down from the kitchen at the rear of the house and Will realises how very hungry he is.

'I've just made some tea and cooked a spot of lunch,' says Aunty. 'I expect you're hungry.'

'Yes, thank you,' says Anna.

'Let's get you sorted, then.'

There is a steaming pot of something bubbling away on the cooker. A transistor radio broadcasts Gracie Fields singing 'Wish me luck', which Aunty starts to sing tunelessly along to. In contrast to what they have seen of the house so far, the kitchen is warm and cosy. Will sees a pistol and a box of bullets lying on a small table and exchanges nervous glances with Anna.

'Sorry, dears, force of habit leaving that lying around,' says Aunty, noticing. She puts the pistol and bullets into a drawer. 'You just never know who might pop by,' she quips. 'Now, sit down and I'll serve up lunch.'

Will notices an unpleasant underlying odour that is only just masked by whatever is cooking in the pot. He looks at Anna, who glances at Aunty, and back to Will with a questioning expression. Will shrugs; he is as confused as she is. He turns to Aunty, 'How did you know we were coming?'

'I heard about the attack at Beaulieu and then caught your distress call. I responded and sent you this address.'

'Do you work for the Secret Service?' asks Anna.

'That's right, dear.'

'What happens now?' asks Will.

'We sit tight and wait for someone to come and pick you up.'

'How long will that take?'

'I couldn't say. We are in a spot of bother as you know.'

'Have you heard from Eoin, or the Major?'

'Nothing yet. Best we just sit tight and wait.'

Aunty serves up greasy corned beef fritters with bread and dripping and three mugs of strong tea. Will's growing anxiety about Eoin dampens his appetite, but nevertheless he eats, knowing he needs to keep his strength up. Despite its appearance, the meal is delicious.

Chapter 25

The Trapdoor

Will sits next to Anna at the kitchen table, reading the book on Greek mythology.

'Listen to this,' he says. 'The Greek god of war, Ares, was given a stone of great power by his lover, Aphrodite. It was known as the Firestone and was a jewel of the finest blue sapphire. It was embedded into his shield – when struck in battle, the jewel would emit a fierce lightning and strike down his foes. Many died horrible deaths. Eventually, Ares was slain in battle by the spear of Diomedes. The same spear was used to destroy the Firestone. Only it didn't destroy the Firestone, it merely shattered it into twelve different-coloured rocks.'

Will opens the notebook and turns to a page depicting a map of the Mediterranean. There is thick grey line charting the journey from Greece to Egypt. 'If the notebook is correct, these same rocks might somehow have shown up in Egypt many years later.'

He flicks through the pages of the notebook and stops at the sketch of the high priest, Aaron. 'There are twelve rocks on Aaron's breastplate of judgement, which some believe had a *divine* power. Seems a strange coincidence.'

'It all seems to be so far-fetched,' says Anna.

'I thought so, too, but I have seen a fragment of these rocks and felt its power.'

'But you said you didn't believe they could cause fire.'

Guilt swarms through Will. 'I'm sorry. I just thought the less people know the better.'

'People! Don't you trust me, Will?'

'Yes, of course I do!'

Will is unsure if Anna is angry or hurt that he held this information back.

'We are in this together now, Will. It's my life on the line too. No more secrets, no more lies. Promise me?'

'I promise.'

He meets her gaze and holds it and for the first time feels affection for her. She smiles. 'Tell me more.'

Will feels excitement building. 'Perhaps the Firestone was destroyed, but the rocks together can still wield their power.'

'So whoever unites the Stones will have divine God-like power,' says Anna. 'That's correct.'

'And if someone strikes them, that unfortunate person will be destroyed?'

'That's the theory.'

'What if… what if they are in London and a bomb falls on the Stones?'

Anna's question shifts something from the hidden recesses of Will's mind. A memory opens in the blink of an eye. He feels a tightness in his throat, as if it is being squeezed. He swallows, but he knows, he now understands: 'The city will be destroyed. The war will end. All will be lost and VIPER will control the Stones.'

Anna pales. 'This is all so difficult to… swallow.' She stands up and folds her arms. 'I might get some rest, if you don't mind.'

'Of course.'

Anna leaves; he hears her quiet footsteps making their way upstairs to the bedrooms.

It is dark outside and he estimates it must be around eight in the evening. He closes the books and wonders about VIPER. Was it their intention to see London destroyed before they claim the Stones? He wonders what the odds might be of a direct hit, but prefers not to do the maths.

A spider scuttles across the surface of the table, and comes to a halt at the candlestick. The candlelight flickers, casting an amber glow around the kitchen.

There is still no word from the Service or Eoin and Will feels his nerves tense again, and drums his fingers on the table-top. His instincts rattle him and he wonders if Eoin is still alive or if he has been captured and killed.

The spider begins to form a web below the rim of the candlestick. Will's thoughts whirl as he watches its unwavering determination. He sighs, stands up and begins pacing the kitchen, his concerns turning to the safe house and just how safe it is. Bored with his own company, he walks to the living room to speak with Aunty. Perhaps she knows more than she is saying.

She is sitting on an armchair looking through the grey-netted curtains at the empty street outside. Will crosses the room, stands in the recess and watches the cobbled street too.

'How long have you known Eoin?' asks Will.

'I've known him many years. He's a good man, considering his history.'

'What do you mean?'

'He's a rogue and a law unto himself. An ex-Fenian with a shady past, if you know what I mean.'

Will frowns, but says nothing, unsure he even wants to know.

'The Prime Minister likes him and recruited him personally…'

'The Prime Minister?'

'Yes. Eoin has many years' experience behind him. He has skills that many people don't and he is more useful in the fight against VIPER and the Nazis, than against us.'

Will's attention is drawn to a man in an overcoat, who is walking down Abberline Street and glancing at each house he passes. He slows as he approaches number thirteen but, much to Will's relief, he walks on without looking up.

'Do you think he is dead?'

'I doubt that. He has the luck of the Irish, that one,' Aunty snorts.

The living-room door opens and Anna appears. She has changed into black brogues, a man's sweater and trousers, and she is holding a cloth cap.

'There are two men outside,' she says.

'Step away from the window, Will!' demands Aunty, her voice grave.

Will looks out and sees the man with the overcoat standing across the street. But he is not alone. There is another man with him, tall and broad with a thick black moustache: Colonel Frost.

'Time for you to go,' whispers Aunty.

His muscles tightening, Will eases quietly away from the window and stands by Aunty, who is on her feet and ready.

'Into the kitchen. Quickly!' She ushers them both out of the living room.

The candle has melted and the last of the light is flickering to its end. Will blows it out as Aunty pushes the kitchen table across the floor. As Will's eyes adjust to the gloom, he can see a trapdoor where the table had been.

'Gather your things and climb down here,' says Aunty.

Will grabs his shoulder bag and takes out the last remaining rat bomb.

'I'll have that,' says Aunty.

Will does not argue and hands it across.

Stuffing the notebook into his blazer pocket, he hears the clicking sound of a lock being tampered with. He glances towards the front of the house, his heart racing, then quickly pulls up the trap door. A waft of something putrid almost makes him gag. That would account for the smell that hung around the kitchen. There is a small ladder leading into a pit of darkness.

'What's that smell?'

'Never mind,' says Aunty. 'The tunnel will take you to Plumbers Row. Find a place to hide and watch for me. I will meet you there later.'

'Aunty…' Will protests but his words are cut off by the crack of a gunshot, once, then twice. The door is being kicked and forced open.

'Quickly!' says Aunty.

Anna pulls on her cap and tucks her hair inside before climbing down.

The crashing on the front door increases.

'Go!' hisses Aunty.

Will starts to climb down the ladder. Its rungs are damp under his fingers and rough with rust and time. He stops for a moment, looking back at Aunty whose brow is shiny with perspiration.

'If I don't make it call Baker Street on this number.' She hands him a small piece of paper and a purse full of coins.

Will's brow furrows.

'Tell them, the safe house has been compromised. They will get you to safety.'

'But…'

'Don't look back. Just keep going,' she says and closes the trapdoor. Will can feel the vibration as the table and chairs slide back into place. He hears the ticking of the rat bomb, followed by Aunty swearing at her opponents at the top of her voice. There is an explosion followed by a rally of gunfire and Aunty's voice is no longer shouting.

Chapter 26

The Tunnel

The ladder wobbles and dust sprinkles from the trapdoor, coating Will's fringe, eyelashes and lips. He lowers himself down, takes the torch from his pocket and switches it on. The tunnel is narrow, damp and earthy and makes him think of an unfilled grave. He wipes his mouth and eyes with the sleeve of his blazer, coughing and almost gagging. The smell is horrible – as if they are standing in a pit of rotten eggs.

'Aunty?' asks Anna, clearly alarmed about the explosion.

Will shakes his head. 'I don't know.'

For a moment they say nothing, neither wanting to acknowledge what might have happened.

'She'll be fine,' says Anna.

'Of course she will.'

'What is that smell?'

'I don't know. Let's just get out of here.'

They follow the light of the torch through the tunnel. There seems to be no end to it.

Out of the corners of his eyes, Will sees movement on the walls. It makes the hairs on the back of his neck stand on end. He hears a scuttling sound and in the torchlight sees the glint of hundreds of small black eyes, staring back at them.

Rats!

Not clockwork ones, but real rats. Will can't breathe, an inexplicable fear grips him, and he stops. He feels Anna bump into him.

'Will, what's the matter?'

His head begins to swim and a memory stirs: he is cold and locked in a cell. Rats rain from a hole in the ceiling. He is being tested.

'Will?' Anna's voice shakes him from his fugue.

He swallows, edges away from the walls and tries to focus on the route ahead. Something brushes against his feet and then tiny sharp claws began climbing his trousers, pulling at the fabric. He grimaces and bats his trousers with the back of his hand. The rat squeaks in protest.

'What was that?' asks Anna.

'Nothing. We're nearly there.'

'The walls are moving!' says Anna. 'Oh my God, it's rats!'

'They won't harm you. Just keep moving,' says Will, a little unconvincingly he thinks.

The smell is getting worse. He steps on something soft, which crunches and squeals under his feet. His stomach lurches. There are rats on the ground, crowding and shuffling around their ankles. The smell is stronger, he gags and then retches. The passage walls begin moving with increasing intensity, the squeaking grows louder as every rodent warns about the intruders.

Will arches forward and throws up. At his feet several vomit-covered rats feast off what had been his lunch. He shakes, unable to move. On each of his shoulders is a rodent scratching his face reaching for his mouth and whatever sustenance it might bring them. There are others climbing his legs. He must not let this beat him. With three deep breaths, he pulls the rodents from him, tossing them aside. Anna brushes them off her sweater and seems more in control.

'We have to run,' says Will. 'Just run as fast as you can.'

Will points the torch into the distance and runs up the tunnel, ignoring the crunching and squealing underneath his feet.

Ahead he sees a ladder similar to the one under the Abberline Street trapdoor. They hurry toward it with the rats in their wake. Will hands Anna the torch. 'I'll check it's clear first,' he says. She points the narrow beam at the ladder and he climbs up to the top where he discovers a manhole cover.

'Switch off the light.'

The tunnel is plunged into darkness. Will pushes against the heavy steel. The ladder wobbles precariously with the effort but, after a moment, the cover gives and Will peeks outside.

The night air is cool and fresh compared to the horrible stench of the tunnel.

Plumbers Row is a cobbled street full of bombed and burned-out buildings. Rubble is scattered everywhere. Much to Will's relief, it seems to be deserted. Pushing the manhole cover aside, he climbs out and peers down into darkness.

'It's clear,' he whispers.

His eyes sweep the area as he pulls Anna up. At one end of Plumbers Row is a solitary building, still standing amidst the dereliction. A large sign outside reads 'Whitechapel Bell Foundry'. It has survived the bombs and perhaps its luck will rub off on them if they hide there and wait for Aunty.

The side entrance to the foundry has a wooden gate bolted and secured with an oversized padlock that takes Will a few moments to pick open. Behind the gate is the foundry yard, where a huge unfinished bell hangs from scaffolding. On each level of the scaffolding is a platform leading to a balcony with access to the main building. They hurry up the steps to the top platform and a doorway leading to the third floor. The door is unlocked and he steps cautiously into a large room, some sort of workshop that smells of ashes and metal. On one side is an oven and it is full of tables covered with various tools and screws. One squat, arched window with dirty glass has a cricket ball-sized hole in it. Through the hole, he can see along the length of Plumbers Row back towards the tunnel. It is the perfect spot to sit, watch and wait.

Moments pass slowly until finally the manhole cover shifts. Huddled together, cheek to cheek, Will and Anna peer through the small hole in the glass. A broad figures emerges from the ground.

But something is not quite right.

'No…' whispers Anna.

It is not Aunty.

It is Frost.

Chapter 27

The Bell Foundry

Anna backs away and Will too retreats from the window, allowing himself enough distance to watch Frost without being seen. Aunty must be dead. Frost is scanning the area. He looks in the direction of the bell foundry, first at the gate and then up to the window where Will stands rooted to the spot.

Will swallows, but does not move.

Despite the darkness, Will swears he can see Frost smile as he walks towards the entrance to the yard.

Will looks around for an escape route but there is none. The only way out is the way they came in. He has to think. He goes out onto the platform and, over the top of the bell, he sees the gate opening. They are done for. Hurrying back inside he scans the tables for a weapon. Anna has picked up a hammer. But using tools as weapons against guns won't help them for long. Will has an idea. It seems stupid and dangerous but what choice do they have? He picks up some of the heaviest screws.

'Do you have a handkerchief?' he asks.

Anna produces one from her sleeve. Will takes it and begins tearing it up. He whispers the plan and, to his surprise, she agrees. She looks at him and smiles, almost fearlessly.

'Easy.'

Her confidence spurs him on and they slip cautiously out onto the scaffolding platform. He can see Frost below with a pistol in his hand, searching the yard. Will tosses the screws into the air and they scatter across the ground. Frost spins on his feet pointing his pistol first in one direction then another.

Will signals to Anna and she moves across to the other side of platform behind the bell. The platform boards creak and Will sees Frost looking up in their direction. Frost begins climbing the steps, his pistol pointing towards them. Will dips back into the shadows and waits.

It is only moments, but it seems like forever before Will hears Frost approach, his large frame moving cautiously across the platform.

Hiding in the darkness of the workshop, Will holds his breath. Frost stops at the platform entrance, his gun, a Browning automatic, raised and pointing inside.

Will readies himself but Frost glances to his right. For a moment Will thinks Anna has blown their cover, but then it comes – the thunderous clang of the bell slammed by the hammer. The air vibrates and the platform trembles as Frost covers his ears. Will springs from the shadows, charging towards him. The bell rings again and Frost, searching for the bell ringer, does not anticipate the force of Will as he slams hard into him, driving him to the edge of the platform. The Browning slips from his grasp and clatters against surface of the bell as it falls.

Will tries to pull back but he is too far forward, his upper body hovering dangerously over the precipice. Frost starts to fall but quickly grabs Will's arm and pulls him onto the rough metal of the bell. Together they tumble down, Frost squeezing Will's neck and snarling like an animal.

They hit the lip of the bell, topple over and crash to the ground. Choking and winded, Will lands on top of Frost whose grip has loosened. Will acts fast, lifting his fist ready to slam into Frost's face but the Colonel's head is turned sideways, his eyes closed. For a moment, Will thinks he is dead, but he can see his chest moving.

Will sees the Browning across the yard. Scrambling off Frost he races toward the gun and swings around, pointing the pistol back at his slumped form. Frost remains unconscious, eyes closed. Will hears Anna running down the steps.

'Are you hurt?'

He is bruised and sore, but otherwise alright. 'I'm fine,' he says and allows himself to be helped by Anna out of the bell foundry. They both remove the small pieces of torn handkerchief they had used to protect their ears.

As they make their way down Whitechapel Road, Will checks that they are not being followed, his hand firmly on the gun in his trouser pocket, his eyes wary of passers-by who, thankfully, do not give them a second look. His head is muddled with the events of the evening. They have been lucky again, he thinks. He wonders just how much longer their luck will hold out.

A red double-decker bus pulls up at a nearby stop. Will has no idea where it is going, but it will take them away from the Bell Foundry and Frost, who could wake at any moment. They board the bus and sit together upstairs.

'How are you feeling?' asks Anna.

Will does not want to admit he is terrified, confused and that all he wants is for this nightmare to end. He takes three deep breaths and lets the warmth of the bus calm him. 'Better,' he says.

Anna squeezes his hand and Will is grateful, so grateful, not to be alone.

They sit in silence as the bus makes its way into central London. They are on Oxford Street.

'Let's get out here,' says Will. 'Soho will be busy and we can lose ourselves in the crowd.'

They walk down Dean Street and stop at a café selling Italian coffee. He checks the coins Aunty gave him. There's enough to get some sustenance and later make a call to Baker Street.

Inside the café, American jazz, laughter and cigarette smoke greet them. The people – who seem artistic types, 'the bohemian set' he has somewhere heard about – are relaxed and having fun. The contrast to Will's life over the past few days makes his head spin. It is like a different world.

No one bats an eye at the two young people who have just walked in or seems to notice the curious bulge of the Browning in Will's blazer pocket. Anna finds an empty table in the corner away from the door. An enthusiastic waiter with a shock of dark curly hair and a thick moustache wipes down their table.

'What can I get you?'

'Coffee,' says Anna.

'Si.'

'Coffee, please,' says Will.

'Si, si. Very easy,' he laughs. 'Two coffees coming up.'

'Let me see the notebook, please.'

Will takes it from his pocket and hands it across.

Anna flicks through the pages and opens at a sketch of a robed man holding a disc high above his head. He is standing on a mountaintop. A beam of light shines from the moon straight to the disc. She points at the disc.

'What this chap is holding is…' She flicks through the notebook and opens on a grainy photograph of a circular piece of metal with the constellations engraved upon it. '…is one of these.'

Will studies the photograph of the disc. Like so many other things recently, it seems frustratingly familiar.

'I think it's an astrolabe,' explains Anna. 'It's a sort of tool used for determining the location of the sun and the planets and stars. My guess is the chap in the sketch is using his to find the Stones and I think this photograph is the one that will help us.'

Will feels a surge of excitement. 'Anna, you are a genius! I know I have heard or read about astrolabes, but I can't think where.' He notices a poster on the wall opposite. It is in vivid colours and shows London's pre-war tourist sites. He narrows in on one particular building, an idea dawning. 'That's it,' he says.

'What?'

At that moment, the waiter arrives and places their coffees and some water on the table. 'Grazie,' he says and leaves them again.

'I know where we can find one,' says Will.

Chapter 28

The British Museum

Will and Anna stand in the shadows of the British Museum's forecourt, looking around. He has been here before, but when? His mind swirls; he steadies himself as images flicker in his head like random scenes from a movie. Among the images are astrolabes. Focusing, he pushes through the storm that is his memory, further, deeper until he eventually remembers: it was years ago, perhaps four, he was looking at them curiously, his hands and face pressed up against the glass of the display cabinet, wide like a glass coffin on legs. And there was a man watching him. A man he knows, but cannot place. He concentrates on the memory:

'Do you know what these are?' the man says.

Will shakes his head.

'They're astrolabes.'

Will looks at them. There are several, some made from brass, some silver and some gold. On their faces are maps of the night sky and lots of symbols.

'What are they for?' he asks.

The man smiles conspiratorially. 'One day one of them will help you find a great treasure. One of them will set you free and give you what you most desire.'

Will focuses on his memory of the man and tries to make out his features through the storm. He can see him now. He knows the face. The spectacles. It was …

Will feels something squeeze his arm.

'Will, you're miles away,' says Anna. 'What's wrong?'

He takes a breath and runs his fingers through his hair. 'It's nothing.'

But Will had remembered. Four years ago that man had been little more than a stranger. He looked different then, too. Younger compared to the photo.

It was Timothy Chittlock.

Will's mind reels with questions. Was Eoin right about him being Chittlock's sleeper? It had seemed a ludicrous suggestion, but Will has come to understand that he is no ordinary sixteen-year-old. Chittlock had been laying a path for him. But why? And what did Chittlock mean when he said the Stones would give Will what he most desired? And what of these feelings of grief and anger, which constantly haunt his darkest moments? Where do they stem from? Could they be why he became a sleeper? Finding the Stones seems the only way for him to get any answers. First things first, they must find the astrolabe.

'Will?'

'I'm fine.'

He takes three deep breaths and looks at the front of the museum. It has been mercifully spared by the bombs, for the time being anyway. The rows of columns remain sturdy, though some are charred from blasts that had not quite hit the mark.

There is no one around. It is late and the museum is locked up for the night. They make their way to the front entrance where Will examines the lock but finds it is too big and complex for his picks. They look for another entry point and skirt around to the east wing, darting behind the columns one at a time. He spots a tall sash window, its individual panes protected with anti-blast tape, almost six feet from the ground.

'This should do,' he says, wondering how they can get up there. But Anna already has the answer.

'Lift me onto your shoulders.'

Will crouches underneath the window and Anna straddles his shoulders. 'I'm ready,' she says.

Will pushes up. Anna is surprisingly light and within seconds she is off his shoulders and on to the windowsill.

He hears the crack of breaking glass and is grateful the anti-blast tape has prevented it shattering onto the floor inside. Moments later something falls on his head. It is a thick golden rope, of the kind that might hold back a large curtain. He tests it; it seems secure. He looks up to see Anna beckoning him. He hauls himself up beside Anna.

The museum is vast, dark and empty as if… as if… everything is gone.

'This place looks like it's been cleared of exhibits,' says Anna.

A twinge of anxiety grips him. He hopes they are not wasting their time.

It makes sense, obviously. With London being bombed almost every night, why keep all that precious history on display, waiting for the next attack.

'Hopefully, not everything,' says Will.

'Do you remember where the astrolabes are?' says Anna.

'Unless they have been moved, they should be upstairs.'

Will shines the torch down the main foyer. The narrow beam of light picks out the emptiness. It is spooky – more like a mausoleum than a museum. He leads them across the marble floor, their footsteps echoing in the cavernous hall.

Up the staircase and onto the first floor, he shines the beam into every corner. They run from room to room, opening and closing doors, but all they find is dust. Desperate, Will hurries down to the ground floor, searching everywhere, opening gates and entering every possible room, but there is nothing. Absolutely nothing. He wants to cry out in frustration but instead kicks an old tin bucket that has been left behind by a cleaner. It clangs noisily across the room and Will swears angrily under his breath.

They stand in silence for a moment thinking what to do next. Will hears a creaking sound and then a door closing.

'Who's there?' calls a voice.

Will flicks off the torch.

It is a man, old probably, judging by the gravelly tone. 'I have a weapon and I'll use it,' the man says.

Will and Anna slip deeper into the shadows, crouching down out of sight. As his eyes adjust to the gloom, Will watches a small, trembling figure of a man appear, looking all around him. Will wonders who he is: a cleaner, a night watchman? No, he seems well dressed and has the look of an academic. Could he be the curator? If he is, what is he doing in a museum at this time of night with nothing to curate?

The old man is carrying an overcoat, which he clumsily pulls on before shuffling towards the main foyer, occasionally glancing back in their direction. Will hears a heavy door opening. The sound of distant traffic floats into the museum from outside. Then the door is pulled shut, the heavy lock turns and all is silent.

'That was close,' says Anna.

Will looks in the direction the curator had just come and makes his way cautiously toward it. Underneath a stairwell there is a doorway. He pulls the door open and discovers another wider stairwell leading down to a dark and windowless basement.

'What is this place?' says Anna.

'We'll soon find out.'

Satisfied there is no indication of anyone else being down here, Will switches on the torch. The basement is, in fact, a large office with a bank of filing cabinets along one wall and, in front of them, a mahogany desk covered by a stack of papers. It is cool down here and Will can feel a breeze. He points the beam towards it and sees another doorway on the opposite side of the room. He opens it.

Warm air blasts into his face and with it an age old smell of dust, oil and iron. It is a familiar smell. He shines his torch into the darkness and sees another stairwell, this one leading down into the ground. He hears a familiar rumbling noise in the distance: a tube train. This doorway is the entrance to the Underground. But why have an entrance here of all places?

And then he remembers. The British Museum had an underground station, closed for use in 1933, but still very much here. But what was it used for now? Will's heartbeat quickens. He looks at Anna and smiles.

'I think we might have hit the jackpot.'

Chapter 29

The Astrolabe

Will and Anna make their way down the stairwell and into the deserted Underground station. The stone steps are well-worn and lead to a circular tunnel lined with pale green tiles, that are grubby with age and neglect. The station's name is barely visible underneath the grime.

The passageway down to the platform is narrowed by hardwood boxes, filing cabinets and framed pictures draped in blankets. Will hears the rumble of another train and a blast of air cools his face. At the end of the tunnel, fixed to the wall, is a grey metal box with a lever switch labelled Lights. He pulls the lever and for a moment it seems nothing will happen, but then there is a fizzing and crackling noise and, one by one, the lights along the platform come on.

'Wow,' says Will, rubbing the back of his neck.

'Look at all this stuff,' says Anna.

It is like any other Underground station, except laid out on the platform and track is what seems like all the British Museum's exhibits. There are bookshelves, paintings, Egyptian statues, rows of sarcophagi and mummies. There are Greek statues, Roman busts, Japanese swords and armour, Viking helmets, swords and shields. Hundreds and thousands of years of world history all stored out of harm's way in a disused London Underground station.

This is the jackpot, thinks Will, but not exactly the one he was hoping for.

In here, somewhere, amongst all of this history, is a single astrolabe that he needs to find. A needle in a haystack. The thought of searching through all this stuff is daunting and he has no idea where to start. Lucky for them they have the whole night ahead, but he has the feeling that might not be long enough.

'This might be more difficult, than we think,' says Anna, rather stating the obvious.

Will tries to get his bearings. He glances up and down the tunnel: 'I think this is the eastbound route,' he says.

'I can start here,' says Anna.

'I'll take the westbound and search the adjoining corridors and see what I can find.'

Anna smiles, 'Good luck.'

'Thanks. You too.'

'If I find anything I'll call you,' she says as he makes his way to the other platform.

After almost two hours of searching boxes, Will's task is interrupted by a thudding sound from up above. The walls vibrate and the dust ripples like shifting sand. It is late, and he knows above them, in the skies, the Nazis are dropping bombs. He takes small comfort that they are safe underground and turns his attention to the rows of boxes ahead of him.

He spends another few hours rifling through crates stuffed with straw protecting jewellery, vases, pots, wooden tools, but there are no signs of the astrolabes.

And then, he hears Anna's voice, echoing through the tunnel. 'Will, come quick!'

He runs to eastbound platform. Anna is pulling a blanket from a display cabinet concealed behind four tall blue and white vases. Easing his way through, he sees the cabinet Chittlock had shown him four years earlier.

It contains the same astrolabes: two golden, one silver and three bronze, all the size of plates. But there is a smaller one, made from a dark metal. It is chipped, scorched and worn with age. It looks familiar. Will opens the notebook and compares the photograph with the small dark astrolabe.

Engraved upon it are the planets and the constellations and, around its perimeter, are symbols: eyes, pyramids, scythes, swastikas, daggers and upturned crosses.

'It's the same one, isn't it?' says Anna.

Will smiles, 'Yes. It's the one we are looking for.'

Chapter 30

Memories

The cabinet lock takes seconds to open. Will lifts up the heavy glass lid and takes out the astrolabe. It is cool to the touch and heavier than he expected. He runs his fingers over the battered surface feeling out the symbols as if they might provide some clue to what he should do with it.

'How old do you think it is?' says Anna.

'I don't know. As old as the Stones, I suppose.'

They say nothing for a moment, staring at it in awe. It is ancient and, judging by its scars, it has been through many wars.

The walls and ceiling tremble with the distant thudding of the night-time bombs.

'We should stay here until morning,' says Anna.

Will nods and pulls two blankets from the exhibits.

They sit together on the platform, wrapped in the dusty blankets to keep themselves warm. At last the bombing stops. They pore over the notebook trying to figure out how the astrolabe works, but the etchings reveal nothing. Judging from the sketch of the man holding aloft the astrolabe, they both agree that for the astrolabe to work they must be high up a mountain, when the moon is full.

'London is a little short on mountains,' quips Anna.

Will manages a smile, sighs and continues to flick through the notebook, stopping at a sketch of what looks like an elaborate Greek crucifix, inlaid with jewels. At its centre is an large eye. Will wonders what relevance the crucifix has.

Anna yawns.

'Why don't you get some sleep? I can keep watch,' says Will.

'I'll never sleep down here. It's a little creepy. Besides, we're doing this together, remember?'

Anna's words make him feel warm inside and he is so grateful she is with him. 'Together,' he says and for a moment he wants to tell her how remarkable she is, how much he admires and likes her, but he can't quite muddle the words together. Instead, he manages, 'I'm sorry you got dragged into this.'

'It's what I signed up for.'

She removes the cap from her head and begins combing her fingers through her thick hair. 'I can keep watch if you want to get some sleep.'

'I'm with you. It's not the easiest of places to sleep.'

They say nothing for a moment and then Will speaks. 'Tell me about you. How did you end up at Beaulieu?'

Anna looks away, staring into the middle distance. 'I was born in Paris. My father was British, a writer, my mother was German, and an artist. They were Socialists, and political activists who travelled across Europe waving the flag for Socialism. In 1934, we moved from Poland to live in Berlin. My parents were appalled at the rise of the Nazi Party in Germany. They thought they could help stop it but…' Anna stops talking for a moment, looks away and hugs her knees. '…During the Night of the Long Knives, they were taken from our home and marched outside to a dirty back street. I watched from my bedroom window. Mother, father and other members of the party were lined up and executed by the Secret Police.'

Will swallows, unable to comprehend what it must have been like for young Anna to witness her parents' cold-blooded murder.

'I was put into care in a horrible place and treated no better than a stray dog. And then, I was visited by a man. He was a friend of my father. He brought me back to England and put me into a boarding school and later he recruited me. Revenge for my parents. It was my duty, he told me. Who was I to argue? He had saved me, after all, and I had a lot to thank him for.'

'What was his name?'

'Chittlock. He was a teacher at the school, until recently.'

Will feels a chill to the core. Revenge for her parents' death. His stomach is in knots, his head and heart mixed with emotions that he cannot make sense of. Something in what Anna says seems to ring true for him. Too deep and true for comfort. He doesn't want to search down this memory. It feels too painful.

'Do you hear that?' whispers Anna.

Will can hear a light clattering of footsteps echoing from the passage leading to the eastbound platform. He looks in its direction and freezes. Emerging from the tunnel is a man, dressed in a suit and trilby. The man comes to an abrupt halt and stands perfectly still, staring in shock at the two young people wrapped in blankets and sitting amongst hundreds of unboxed rare and valuable exhibits. 'They're here!' he shouts.

Chapter 31

The Chase

Saturday, 10th May 1941

Will jumps up, stuffs the notebook and astrolabe into his blazer pocket and picks up Frost's Browning. He looks around for an escape route. There is only one.

'We'll have to go through the tunnel,' he says.

Anna nods, grabs the torch and hops onto a sarcophagus resting on the rail track. Will follows and together they slide down to the track below. He glances back at the man who is navigating his way through the scattered exhibits. Anna puts on her cap and tucks her hair inside.

'That's my cover blown,' she says with a wry smile.

'Let's get out of here,' says Will.

They hurry up the uneven, oily surface of the track, into the tunnel where the darkness is absolute. Anna turns on the torch, its beam provides a small amount of light, enough to make their way up the track without tripping over.

Will turns to see the man lowering himself on to the sarcophagus. A second man has joined him. They are both now carrying pistols.

'Run!'

A gunshot echoes through the tunnel, the bullet whistles past them.

'Get down!' says Will.

Another bullet flies dangerously just over their heads. Anna turns off the torch. 'We're sitting targets with this light.'

Their eyes adjust to the gloom and they stumble forward as quickly as they can. Will crouches down as Anna runs ahead, and points the Browning at the silhouetted figures hurrying up the track. The gun is heavy and he trembles, his stomach churning at the thought of what he is about to do. But what choice does he have? It's him and Anna against these men. There is only one choice. He aims the gun, squeezes the trigger and fires. The noise is deafening and the men throw themselves to the ground. Will fires again and again, crying out in anger as he does so. The men do not move but, as far as he can tell, they are unharmed.

He hears them whispering, fires again three times and then runs blindly after Anna. His foot slips on the oily surface and he falls, dropping the Browning, his face slamming against a rusty track. Winded and sore, he stands up, head spinning and hurries on.

'Are you all right?' says Anna.

'Yes.' Although his left cheekbone is throbbing.

The tunnel begins to vibrate and Will sees lights flash by in the distance. There's a train coming. It is later in the morning than he'd thought.

Anna reaches out and holds his hand for support. It is warm and he squeezes it, but not too tightly.

Working together, they navigate the uneven slippery track.

He can hear the men behind them but they don't seem to be gaining ground.

Will can see they are approaching the end of the tunnel, which is blocked with a wire fence. His heart sinks, but suddenly he sees that there is a gap at the top, which they can squeeze through.

Will hears a thud and then one of the men swears. He wonders if he has fallen.

He looks beyond the wire fence. There are lights shining in the adjoining tunnel that provide a small of amount of visibility. The track could be live. They will have to be mindful. He stands with his back to the fence and cups his hands into a footrest.

'Stay clear of the rails. This is probably a working track.'

Anna climbs up and over effortlessly, slipping through the gap in the wire. Will pulls himself up and then looks up the lighted tunnel. He can see the platform ahead, like a porthole in the darkness, with commuters waiting for the next train.

'It's a live track,' says Anna, confirming his suspicions.

By his calculations, it has been a few minutes since the last train. That should give them enough time.

He exchanges looks with Anna who seems to know exactly what he has in mind.

'Ready?' she says.

'Ready.'

They dash up the track as fast as they can, staying clear of the live rails. Will glances behind, hoping the two men are nowhere near the fence yet.

They keep running but something is not quite right. It doesn't seem to be getting closer. A horrible thought occurs to him. He has made a terrible error. He swallows. In the depths of the underground, in the narrow dark tunnels, determining the distance of an endpoint accurately is more difficult than above ground. How could he be so stupid?

There is still no sign of a train. How long has it been since the last one? He estimates minutes, perhaps three, but that was wishful thinking. It was six minutes, maybe even more. That would mean… and then he hears it. The air trembles and the track vibrates. Will's heart begins to pound.

Anna has heard the train and increases her pace. She is almost six feet ahead of him

The train rumbles in the distance and spurs Will on faster.

The weight of the astrolabe slams against his side, his arms are wide, pumping the air and providing the balance needed for the uneven surface.

The rumbling is now a rapid rattling of steel on steel, wheels racing over tracks. Will glances behind him and sees the light of the train, small but growing. Its distance is impossible to determine. *Run. Just run.*

He can see Anna near the entrance to the platform. 'Hurry,' she shouts.

Will can feel the train speeding toward them. He turns to see the driver's face. He is yawning and oblivious to the young people on the track ahead. Will sprints forward toward the light, no longer a porthole but the entrance to Holborn station. He hears shouts from the commuters but ignores them. Anna has swung up to the platform, helped by some of the travellers. Will can feel the wind of the oncoming train. He reaches for the edge of the platform but he is weak and tired and loses his grip.

'What the bloody hell are you two playin' at?' says a voice.

With his very last ounce of strength, he pulls himself onto the platform and lies on his back, gasping for breath as the train speeds into the station.

Chapter 32

The Lovebirds

As soon as Will is able to stand, they run to the exit, ignoring the glares of disapproval from the people on the platform. Will's heart thuds against his chest as if it is trying to beat its way out of the confines of his tired and sore body. With their heads down, and not enough money, they race through the turnstiles, passing a guard who shouts for their tickets.

Outside, the street is bustling. The morning air cools Will's face as they hurry away from the station. Keep moving; they have to keep moving but where should they go? Baker Street is the obvious choice, however, the agents of VIPER, or the Pastor, might be watching out for them. He looks west down High Holborn. He thinks they should just keep going until they come up with a place to in which to base themselves and then make the call to Baker Street.

Anna loops her arm in his as they cut across to Newton Street, which has seen the worst of the previous night's air raid. Dust and smoke choke the air. Firemen are hosing down the last of the flames.

A policeman, wearing a protective tin hat, is standing close by watching them work. Will and Anna keep a low profile and pick their way over the rubble holding hands to keep each other steady. Anna's flat cap is pulled over her head with her hair tucked inside. Dressed like a boy and walking with a swagger, Will has to check twice it is actually her and not some strange bloke.

''Ere! You two. Wot you doin' there?'

Will's heart sinks. The policeman is beckoning them over.

'Come 'ere,' he says, frowning.

Will and Anna exchange nervous glances and realise they are still holding hands while Anna is dressed as a young man. Anna's grip on Will's hand loosens.

'Wot's keepin' ya?' says the copper.

They make their way toward him, Will steadies his breathing and smiles warmly. 'Sorry constable, we were a little distracted.'

'What do you mean distracted? What you doing hanging about 'ere, holding hands like that? It ain't right!'

'I'm sorry, officer, we were…'

'Where's your gas masks?' he says, interrupting him.

'We lost them,' says Will.

'You lost 'em!' said the policeman, his voice rising in pitch.

'No, we didn't, Tommy,' says Anna. 'We left them at home, remember?'

Will glances at Anna, her eyebrows arch as she looks at him.

'Oh yes,' he says realising the ruse. 'We left them at home and we are just going back to get them now just in case a gas bomb explodes and…'

The officer points at Will's blazer pocket. 'You forgot your gas masks but not those. Wot's in your pockets, then?'

'Just a book and… erm… nothing important.'

'I'll be the judge of that,' says the policeman, holding out his hand.

For a moment Will thinks to run but they would never make it across the rubble, not the two of them. He hands across the notebook and astrolabe and considers how to knock the policeman out without attracting attention.

The policeman leafs through the notebook and glances suspiciously at Will and Anna. He then examines the astrolabe. 'Wot's this then?' he says, holding it up.

'Erm… It's for a project I'm working on,' says Will.

'What sort of project?' says the policeman, studying the astrolabe with interest. 'It looks old, as if it should be in a museum.'

'I don't know about that,' says Will, with a nervous laugh. His hand curls into a fist and at that same time he hears sniffing. He turns to see Anna holding her cap in her hands, head bowed, shoulders shaking.

'Blimey,' says the policeman, 'he's a girl!'

The policeman looks at Will, his eyes wide.

Will shrugs.

'Wot's the matter?'

'We're on our way to hospital to visit my grandfather,' says Anna. 'His street was all but destroyed in the air raid. He was one of the few survivors, but they don't reckon he has all that long… to go.' Anna starts sobbing, takes out a handkerchief and wipes real tears from her eyes. Will puts his arms around her shoulders and wonders how she can do that.

'Oh my word,' says the policeman, handing the astrolabe and notebook back. 'You should have said sooner.'

The policeman's gaze lingers on Will for a little longer than is comfortable. 'Do I know you?' he asks, with a frown.

'No, sir, I don't believe we have met.' Will looks away and tries to sound as polite as he can. 'We should really get going.'

'Yes, you two lovebirds get off to the hospital and see the old fella.'

Lovebirds?

Will smiles and notices Anna blushing. Will pretends he did not hear what the policeman said.

They thank him and then hurry off across the rubble, but Will can still feel him watching them. His face is obviously still familiar from the newspapers. Could the police still be looking for him? He doesn't want to think about it. They were lucky to get past this copper who has clearly not been paying attention to the papers. They may not be so lucky next time.

'We need to find a telephone box. Aunty gave me the Baker Street code.'

Anna seems quiet and he wonders if the lovebirds comment has bothered her. Without saying much they search the streets and eventually find a phonebox on Charing Cross Road.

Will drops the remaining pennies into the slot and dials the operator.

'Operator, how may I help you?'

'Baker Street 0764'

'Putting you through.'

The phone rings for a few moments and is answered by a man's voice. 'Hello.'

Will hesitates before answering. The voice seems familiar, but he cannot be certain. He glances at Anna who is scanning the area, checking they are not being watched.

'The safe house has been compromised. Aunty is dead.'

There is silence for a moment.

'Who is this?'

'My name is Will Starling. I'm with Anna Wilder. We are agents from Beaulieu. We need to come in.'

'Where are you, Will?'

'Charing Cross Road.'

'Find somewhere quiet and out of the way. I will come and find you.'

'What's your name?'

'Dalton.'

The name echoes at the back of his mind and niggles.

'Where can I find you, Will?'

Will sweeps his hand through hair, thinking, and then remembers the perfect place. 'Fenchurch Street. There is a disused bus repair yard. You can find us there.'

'Good. Stay out sight and I will find you.'

Will places the receiver down and frowns. *Dalton. Why does that name sound familiar?*

Chapter 33

Fire and Brimstone

They make their way to Fenchurch Street, then up the alley and stand at the tall wooden doors, the entrance to the yard. There is no one around and it is strangely quiet. The hatch is ajar, which seems odd.

Will pushes it open.

The place looks just the same as when he left it, with the old bus, home for Kitty and her gang, and the makeshift table, covered in the previous night's haul of food. It is deathly quiet. Will feels a fluttering in his stomach. There is no one here.

'Hello!' he calls, his voice echoes unanswered.

Anna walks ahead of him, 'Hello!'

But there is no response.

And then Will hears a yelp from inside the bus. He holds his breath and looks at Anna, who returns his gaze. Something is wrong. They both know it.

They walk towards the bus and Will pulls the red velvet curtain across. Inside the cushions are torn and strewn across the floor. He sees a lone shoe amongst them, then the person it belongs to lying flat out on the floor, eyes closed and nose bloody. It is the freckled boy with the machete, which he still grips firmly in his hand. His chest is moving – he is still alive.

He sees Kitty sitting nearby him. She is hugging her knees and trembling, her eyes red raw with tears.

Then he sees Sam.

He is shaking, his eyes wide with fear, a golf ball-sized bruise on his jaw. A black-gloved hand holds his forehead back and a long thin blade lies against his exposed throat.

'Hello. I knew you'd come back,' says the Pastor, in clipped tones.

Will feels his spine icing over. 'Let him go.'

'Come come. First things first. You know what I want.'

Will levels his gaze with the Pastor's dark, soulless eyes. They flash for a moment and Will could swear they turn red as the blade of his white knife presses into Sam's flesh. A droplet of blood rolls down the boy's neck.

Will feels a rising rage, but fights to keep calm. 'Let him go.'

'The notebook.' says the Pastor, firmly.

'The notebook is nothing. It has served its purpose. I have the Stones. I can give them to you,' he lies.

The Pastor appraises him. 'Show them to me.'

'They're not here.'

The Pastor sighs.

'Why do you want them?' asks Will, trying to buy some time before Dalton arrives.

'Show them to me,' replies the Pastor.

Will's skin prickles. How long can he delay him? 'Why do you want something that is clearly an instrument of the devil? Is he your god now? Is it Satan you worship?'

The Pastor's eyes flare and bore into Will's. He has rattled him.

'There is no shame, Pastor. Satan holds all the power, after all.'

The Pastor chuckles darkly. 'Young man, you have quite the tongue. I shall enjoy cutting it from your mouth.'

'You will never have that opportunity.'

The Pastor shakes Sam. 'Show me the Stones.'

'I told you, I don't have them with me.'

The Pastor tugs roughly at Sam's head and presses the blade further into his flesh. Sam whimpers as more blood gathers beneath it and flows like a red tear down his neck.

Will steps forward, his hands raised. 'No… wait… I can take you to them.'

'You're lying,' growls the Pastor.

'If you kill him, you will not see me or the Stones.'

'You will not escape me, boy.'

'Do not underestimate me, Pastor.'

'Do not underestimate me, boy.'

Will stands firm and feels Anna close by. Then, out of the corner of his eye, he sees the freckled boy move. Is he awake? Will's gaze remains on the Pastor's cold eyes.

And then he hears a hard thud. The Pastor's face contorts in pain as the freckled boy slams the machete into his shin. Will lunges for the Pastor's knife hand, grabbing his wrist until it bends backward to breaking point. Anna surges forward and launches her fist hard at his temple. The Pastor stumbles back, the knife slipping from his grasp. Anna kicks it across the floor and out of the bus.

Sam crawls toward Kitty, who has not moved.

Will turns to Kitty, Sam and the freckled boy. 'Get out of here!' he shouts.

They scuttle from the bus without hesitation.

Adrenalin pumps through Will's body. His rage surges forward and with Skipper's murder, and the threat to Sam, at the forefront of his mind, he slams his fists without conscience. The Pastor falls back to the floor with Will on top of him thrashing him repeatedly. A black cloud darkens Will's mind; he cannot stop.

The Pastor lies still, but Will rages on.

Anna touches Will's shoulder: 'That's enough, Will. He's finished.'

The Pastor's eyes are closed, his lips and nose bloody.

Will is panting, his heart pumping like an out of control steam train. A primal urge sweeps through him, old, savage and unrecognisable. Kill him, finish him, his instincts tell him. Looking down, he sees the Pastor's bloodied lips part in a smile, his teeth tinged red, his hollow black eyes giving him the appearance of a sinister and mad clown. Some fragment of humanity makes Will pause. And as he does, the Pastor's hands reach for Will's throat and squeeze tightly.

'He will be tormented with fire and brimstone in the presence of the holy angels and in the presence of the Lamb…'

Will tries to pull the hands away, but the grip is firm.

'…And the smoke of their torment goes up forever and ever; and they have no rest day and night, those who worship the beast and his image, and whoever receives the mark of his name.'

The Pastor gets to his feet holding Will by the throat as if he is a lifeless dummy.

Anna runs at the Pastor but he pushes Will forward using him like a battering ram. Will can feel Anna behind him, her hands reaching in vain for the Pastor as he pushes them both hard against the side of the bus. Anna cries out in pain and slides to the floor.

Will claws at the Pastor's face, kicking hard at his legs, but it seems to have no effect. It is as if he is immune to pain. The Pastor carries him across the room, and slams him into the bus windows. Will's body crunches painfully against the glass, which cracks on impact. He can't focus, his head begins to spin and darkness beckons. The Pastor laughs and tosses him across the inside of the bus. A window shatters, Will falls to the ground, fragments of glass fall on top of him, cutting his hands and face. Pain sears through his body, he groans, powerless and weak as the Pastor straddles him and grips his throat, squeezing the breath from him.

Parts of Will's life, a life lost in the mists of his memory flash before him: a terrible loss – the murder of his family. He cannot remember their faces but he feels the gaping loss. Something in his soul has died and at the core of his heart is the need for vengeance. Tears prick the back of his eyes.

The Pastor squeezes tighter. Will chokes and gasps for breath, his face burning and rushing with blood. It is all about to end. When he dies, the Pastor will kill Anna, Sam, Kitty and the other lost children.

He cannot let that happen.

Will's arms thrash on the floor, his hands searching for something, anything. The Pastor stares down at him, waiting for that final second when Will's life will leave his eyes.

The darkness is getting closer. *No. No. Not like this.* Will's fingers brush the edge of something sharp, a thick shard of glass. He shuffles it into his palm, squeezing hard on the edges and slicing open his skin.

His vision is blurring. With a final ounce of strength he plunges the shard blindly at the Pastor. The Pastor screams and his grip on Will's neck loosens. He gasps for breath, coughing uncontrollably, his lungs filling gloriously with air. Scrambling back, he pushes himself quickly into a standing position, but his head is light and he is unsteady on his feet.

The Pastor is on his knees crying and trembling, his hands hovering over the shard that is lodged in his right eye. Will grimaces and skirts around him leaning on the side of the bus for support.

Anna is clutching her side, her face ashen. Dizzy and in pain, Will helps her up and they stumble out of the bus. Wills sucks in the cool refreshing air. The Pastor screams once more. Will shudders and follows Anna through the hatch in the gates. Together they run down the alleyway towards Fenchurch Street.

Chapter 34

The Greek Cross

Running down Fenchurch Street, Will catches sight of a green Humber parked at the side of the road. Resting against it is a red faced and panting Sam. He is talking to a man with slicked back blond hair, dressed in a dark blue suit. Kitty and the freckled face boy are nowhere to be seen.

The man watches Will and Anna approach.

'Sam?' says Will, narrowing his gaze at the man in the suit.

The man interjects, 'Will Starling?'

'Dalton?'

The man nods and smiles thinly.

'We have to get out of here quickly,' says Will, glancing back in the direction of the yard. There is no sign of the Pastor. Yet. He opens the rear doors of the car. 'Get in Sam. You're coming with us.'

'Bleedin' hell. Who was he?' says Sam, rubbing his neck.

'A bad man. Are you hurt?' says Will.

'I'm chipper,' says Sam, but Will can hear a tremor in his voice. Sam jumps into the passenger seat and looks back at Will with a worried expression.

Dalton gets into the driver seat and looks distastefully at Will's bloody hand. 'Try not to bleed all over my car,' he says.

Will furrows his brow and studies Dalton's face. 'Have we met?'

'No,' says Dalton easing off the brakes and shifting gears. The Humber moves forward and picks up speed. They pass the yard. Will glances at the doors. There is no sign of the Pastor. He turns to Anna who is gently dabbing Sam's neck with a handkerchief.

'Anna, meet Sam,' he says.

'Hello Sam.'

'Enchanté, Miss, enchanté,' he says, bowing his head slightly.

Anna smiles and looks at Will.

'Are you hurt, Anna?' he says.

'Bruised jaw and ribs. All in a day's work. Not as bad as you. We need to stem the flow of blood.' She removes her jumper and tears off the sleeve from her shirt, wrapping the cloth tightly around Will's palm. He winces as the binding tightens.

'Sorry,' says Anna.

Sam sits quietly, hugging his arms. 'Lucky you came along when you did, Will. I thought he was going to kill us.'

'I'm glad you're safe, Sam, but this is not over yet.'

Dalton seems to be taking them towards the river and the north Thames Embankment, or so Will thinks, but instead he turns down Tanner Lane and along the road between the warehouses and the waterside. They drive slowly over rubble, passing several bomb-damaged warehouses that are beyond repair. The car stops beside a postbox, opposite an old shipping warehouse called Butler's Wharf. Dalton gets out of the car and Will and the others follow. Holding his bloody hand close to his side, Will looks around him. To the west, busy on either side with queuing traffic, is Tower Bridge. It was there, almost a week ago, that he witnessed Skipper's murder at the hands of the Pastor.

Across the water is the north of the city with its crumbling war-torn cityscape. He can see some of the churches mentioned in the 'Oranges and Lemons' rhyme and towering over them is St Paul's Cathedral flanked by two enormous barrage balloons. Somewhere out there, he thinks, are the Stones of Fire. They are close. He knows it.

Dalton escorts them inside the unused warehouse. They are led up a flight of stairs to a room with tall windows overlooking the river. There is a long metal table near the window with a bench on either side.

'Get some rest. Help will be here soon,' says Dalton, turning to leave.

'Are you leaving us?' says Will.

'I'll be outside, if you need anything,' he says, closing the door behind him.

Will has an uneasy feeling and opens the door to look outside. There is a bitter smell of tobacco in the air. Dalton is sitting on an old office chair, leaning against the wall, puffing on a cigarette. He looks back at Will, curiously. Will says nothing, dips back inside and closes the door. After all that has happened, it is hard to know when he might be overreacting.

'What's going on Will? What's this all about?' asks Sam.

Will smiles at Sam. What harm could it do to tell him? He deserves the truth after what he has been through, Will thinks. He starts to give Sam a potted summary of the last few days.

'I knew you was someone important, Will. I told Kitty, but she didn't believe me.'

'I'm not important, Sam. I'm just trying to do the right thing.'

Sam looks at Anna and then back at Will. Folding his arms, he says, 'You is too humble, Will. You are more important than you think.'

Will shrugs and tries to smile. He takes out the astrolabe and the notebook and places them on the table. 'Let's try and figure out some more of this puzzle.'

Leafing through the pages, he begins tearing them out. First, the picture of the cross, followed by the sketch of the man holding up the astrolabe on the mountain. He lays them out on the table and runs his fingers through his hair. 'Ouch,' he says, his finger grazing a piece of glass.

He eases it out and drops it on the floor. Anna stands behind him. 'Let me,' she says and tips his head gently to the side. 'It's a mess. I'll see if I can get some water.'

She stands in the doorway, speaks with Dalton briefly and then looks back inside. 'Be back shortly.'

Will and Sam sit at the table and look down at the pictures.

'Somewhere in here,' says Will, 'is the final piece of the puzzle. The Stones of Fire are somewhere in London.'

Will recalls the churches from 'Oranges and Lemons' and glances through the window and beyond the river. 'Could they be in one of those churches?' he wonders aloud.

'Which one?' says Sam.

'That's what we need to figure out.' Will looks down at the etching of the cross. The design is elaborate, thick and broad with short rounded arms and a rectangular base. Within its frame are rows of neatly arranged rectangles and circles. Encrusted jewels, he suspects, and in its centre, is what looks like the pupil of an eye. Will does not know what to make of it. He hands the etching to Sam. 'What do you think this is?'

Sam studies it. 'It looks familiar,' he says.

'Really? Keep looking and think hard, Sam. You could save all our lives.'

The door opens and Anna walks in cradling a basin, with water sploshing from it. Draped over her arm is the remains of her shirt, torn into rags. She sets the basin on the table and slides along the bench, sitting next to Will. She dips one of the rags in the water. 'This might hurt a little,' she says.

Evening comes and the moon is full and low and casts a mercurial sheen across the city rooftops. Will winces as Anna removes yet another piece of glass from his head, a task that has taken almost two hours. With the aid of his torch and a lock pick, she removes the more stubborn pieces and wipes the small wounds with a rag dipped in the bloodied water.

'That's the last of them,' she says.

Will's head throbs, it has been like torture and he is relieved it is over.

'Sorry, it was a little horrible for you,' she says, fixing his hair.

'It wasn't too bad,' he lies. 'Thank you.'

Will feels Sam watching him. Sam winks and silently mouths, 'Aye, aye.'

Will glowers and turns back to the pictures spread out in front of him. He focuses hard: the Greek cross, the mountain, the astrolabe, the moon. What does it all mean?

He looks at Anna and Sam. 'If the Stones are in London, what mountains are there to climb and hold the astrolabe high up?'

'None,' says Anna.

'Correct. So what is the next best thing?'

'Somewhere very high up,' offers Sam.

'Yes, but where?' Will stands up and paces for a moment before walking to the window. He glances nervously at the moon, now swathed in charred clouds. Tonight is their only hope. They cannot afford to wait for the next cycle.

'We have to find them and get them out of London. Tonight, if we can,' says Will.

The wail of a siren shatters the silence. An air raid! The hairs on Will's neck stand on end. He looks out the window and across the river. Small dark figures are hurrying to the safety of the shelters as the crump, crump, crump of bombs explode further east.

Searchlights slice through the sky looking for enemy aircraft. One beam swipes across St Paul's and lights up the golden ball and cross that rise up above the dome.

Will runs his fingers through his hair. Something tugs at his memory. He turns to the table, grabs the picture of the cross and looks at it, then back at the cathedral. He searches the recesses of his mind. He knows this cross. He looks across the water and laughs to himself.

'Of course,' he says. 'That's it.'

'What's it?' says Anna.

'This is not a Greek cross. It's a floor plan.'

'For where?' says Anna.

'St Paul's Cathedral,' says Sam. 'I knew I'd seen it before.'

'Exactly,' says Will, turning and looking across the water at the great cathedral. 'That's where we have to go next.'

As if on cue, the clouds part revealing the moon. The city seems to shimmer dangerously in preparation for the destruction that is only minutes away.

'Look!' says Sam, pointing at the table.

Will follows his gaze and sees small blue lights like miniature fireworks spiral across the astrolabe. It is the strangest thing.

'What's happening?' says Anna.

'Blimey!' says Sam.

'The Stones really are close,' says Will.

'But how can you be sure?' said Anna.

'The astrolabe is a device for finding them. It defies all logic, but the full moon has activated it.'

His heart starts racing. 'We should get out of here,' he says, tentatively reaching for the astrolabe, his fingers brushing the lights. There is no heat and it seems safe. He takes a breath and then picks it up. The lights are cool to the touch and spread across his hands and wrists. It is almost hypnotic. With precious little time, he shoves it into his pocket, grabs the notebook and the torn-out pages.

Anna and Sam are already at the door. Sam is pulling at the handle.

'The door's locked,' he says.

Anna tries to open it, but it is no good.

Will hears the sound of a car engine and hurries to the window. A car has pulled up beside the Humber. Dalton is standing close by as if waiting to greet whoever is inside. The doors open and two broad men wearing suits get out from the rear. They look to Will like heavies. A third man, who is thin and balding with spectacles, gets out. It is the librarian from Bishopsgate Library. *What is he doing here?* And then a fourth man follows and looks up at Will with a grim smile. Will feels his muscles coil.

It is Colonel Frost.

Chapter 35

Flight from Butler's Wharf

'Will!' cries Anna. 'Help us open the door.'

Will's eyes dart around the room, searching for another exit, an escape route that he may have missed, but there is nothing. They are trapped.

'Come away from the door,' he says.

Anna and Sam look at him with questioning expressions.

'What is it, Will?' demands Anna.

'Dalton has tricked us. He's a double agent.'

Anna's face pales.

Sam presses his ear to the door. 'Someone's coming up the stairs.'

Anna and Sam stand beside Will.

The lock turns and the door is pushed open. The two heavies enter with pistols pointing firmly at Will.

Will takes three deep breaths.

Frost steps in, walks between his men and crosses the room, his face grim and his fists clenching in and out as if he is preparing for a fight. He is a beast of a man, remarkably unharmed after his fall at the bell foundry. It will obviously take a lot more than a fall to down this monster.

Will can feel Sam shrink behind him.

Frost stands before Will and stares deeply into his eyes.

'Well, if it isn't the prodigal son.'

Will can feel his heartbeat quickening.

'You've had quite the adventure, my boy.'

Will bristles. 'I'm not your boy.'

'Not any more…' Frost runs his eyes greedily up and down Anna. Looking back at Will, he says, 'You have good taste.'

Will eyes flare in anger.

Outside the siren continues to wail, lights flash in the sky and the falling bombs draw closer. Frost turns his head and calls to the librarian who stands sheepishly in the doorway.

'Mr Stringer, join us, please.'

The librarian hesitates and then steps cautiously into the room. 'I really ought to be going now,' he mumbles 'It is rather late and mother will be worried.'

'A moment of your time. That is all.'

Stringer clasps his hands together and turns to leave, but Dalton steps in his path. He reluctantly approaches, eyes down.

'Look at them,' says Frost. 'Do you recognise them?'

Stringer nods and then points to Sam. 'Not that one.'

Frost looks warily at Sam.

Will shifts uneasily and Frost catches his discomfort in the blink of an eye.

'And what were they doing at the library, Mr Stringer?'

'Researching history. Greek history and the Renaissance period, a speciality subject of mine, actually. I…'

'Researching history,' interrupts Frost. 'Quite.' He looks at the notebook in Will's hand. 'William, I presume you have made some headway on finding the location of the Stones?'

Will swallows, but does not respond.

'As I thought.'

'May I go now?' Stringer says with a tremble in his voice.

Frost continues to stare at Will and ignores Stringer. 'I don't blame you for what you did. Considering your circumstances, I would have done the same.'

Will swallows. He does not know why, but somewhere in his fractured memory is a dark truth, that he does not want to face. He breathes slowly through his nose and retains his composure.

'Colonel, may I go?' says Stringer.

'This is a free country, is it not?' says Frost.

Stringer nods, backs away and then stops. He coughs politely, 'There was a small matter of remuneration.'

'About that…' says Frost, reaching into his coat pocket and pulling out a pistol.

Instinctively, Will and Anna duck, pulling Sam with them. The shot is explosive, the bullet hits Stringer in the centre of his forehead. A spray of blood splashes across Dalton's face as Stringer crumples to the ground.

Sam cries out and Anna puts her arm around him and pulls him to her.

'Where are the Stones, William?'

Will is breathing deeply, trying to hide his terror. 'I should have finished you off at the bell foundry.'

'Your mistake. Didn't you learn anything from me? Now, tell me where are the Stones. If you do not, I will kill your friends one by one until you do.'

Will's mind is racing. He and Anna cannot take them all on.

'You,' Frost gestures at Sam. 'Come here.'

Trembling, Sam looks down at the floor.

Frost sighs impatiently. 'Wykes, fetch the boy.'

One of the heavies grabs Sam by the arm and hauls him from Anna's clutches.

'Hey!' cries Will. He rushes forward and pulls Sam back, but a firm grip takes hold off his hair and he can feel Dalton's gun barrel against his temple.

'On your knees, little one,' says Frost.

Sam is too frightened to move. Wykes kicks his legs from underneath him and Sam falls at Frost's feet. He raises the pistol.

'One by one, William.'

'Tell them Will,' cries Anna.

Will feels a crushing panic as Frost squeezes the trigger.

'St Paul's Cathedral!' he says. 'They are in St Paul's Cathedral.'

Frost looks through the window and across the river at the great cathedral. 'You will have to do better than that, Will.'

'I don't know where precisely but I can find them, I swear. Please don't hurt him.'

Frost smiles, clearly enjoying Will's fear and pleading.

'He's telling the truth!' says Anna, 'Please...'

After a moment, Frost puts the pistol back in his coat pocket.

'Very well. I will give you the benefit of the doubt. We shall make the journey to St Paul's together.'

Frost walks to the window and takes out a torch and binoculars from his coat pocket. He begins to flick the torch on and off, signalling to someone. Will watches as Frost peers through binoculars at two tiny blinking lights on Tower Bridge.

Anna has a better view and is trying to interpret the message. After a moment, she frowns, looks at Will and shakes her head.

Wykes leads the way downstairs followed by Anna, Sam and Will. Dalton, the other heavy and Frost follow behind with their guns ready.

At the bottom of the stairs Wykes stops and raises his arm. Will can hear the sound of a clattering and creaking vehicle approaching. It sounds familiar. Wykes approaches the door and opens it.

Dalton pulls Anna and Sam into the shadows. Frost squeezes Will's shoulder and jabs his ribs with the barrel of his gun. 'Do not open your mouth, or try any of your tricks.'

Through the gap in the door Will sees the vehicle drive past. It's wobbling and trembling are unmistakable. It's Eli's old post-office van. The van stops at the nearby postbox. Will hears the van door opening. Someone is whistling and then: 'Nice evening for an air raid,' says a voice. It is Eoin, but he is speaking in a cockney accent. Will holds his breath and exchanges glances with Anna in the gloom.

'Late to be picking up the mail,' says Wykes.

'People still send letters, even in wartime, mate,' says Eoin, in a jovial tone. 'Those people are working you into the ground.'

'We all have to do our bit.'

Will hears the creaking sound of a door opening. The postbox. There is a shuffling noise and then it slams shut.

'I'll be off then.'

'Goodnight,' says Wykes.

Will tenses and Frost tightens his grip.

The van starts up and drives off. Why is he leaving? Eoin must know they are here.

Moments later the sound of the van disappears into the night swallowed by the drone of approaching bombers.

'Start walking,' says Frost.

Outside the searchlights swing through the skies like swords in battle. Whistlers fall from the bombers and hit the ground without exploding. Time bombs, thinks Will. Tonight, London would become a minefield.

'Colonel,' says Wykes, pointing back in the direction where they had entered the wharf, 'There is another message.'

Frost frowns and eases his grip on Will's shoulder. 'It can't be,' he says, looking through the binoculars. 'I don't recognise the code.'

Will looks at Anna. She has understood it.

'Agents of Beaulieu. Duck!' she whispers.

Is the message from Eoin? It must be. Wisps of smoke are escaping from the slot in the postbox.

Anna pulls Sam to the ground. Will drops too, covering his ears, as an explosion rocks the ground and fills the air with masonry, smoke and dust.

There is a moment of quiet calm before the groaning and swearing starts.

Will coughs and looks up. Clouds of black smoke swirl from the decimated pillar-box. At ground level, the smoke is thin and he can just about make out Anna and Sam. They seem unhurt.

'Hold hands. We're getting out of here,' says Will. The smoke is thickening. There is no sign of Frost, or his men, but he can hear them shifting close by.

The bomb was small, more diversion than destruction. Will covers his mouth to stave off the thick, black choking air and leads his friends away from the warehouse groping the walls for support and searching for a way out.

A gunshot rings out, piercing the smoke above their heads. It is followed by the sound of heavy footfalls close behind.

Someone is following them.

Chapter 36

The Light That Had Seemed So Bright

Will blinks the smoke from his streaming eyes and covers his mouth with the sleeve of his jacket. He can feel Anna's soft hand holding on tightly to his. An image from the past flashes in his mind. He stops, tightens his grip and recalls a small hand holding tightly on to his. But the image dissipates as quickly as it arrived.

Whose hand was that?

He pulls Anna forward and she in turns pulls a coughing and choking Sam.

'Cover your nose and mouth with something,' Will rasps, his voice almost inaudible. He presses on, pulling them all behind him. Reaching forward, his fingers graze the rough bricks of a warehouse building. Using it as a guide he leads them through the black fog away from Frost and his men.

The smoke begins to thin and he pulls them clear. There is precious little time, but they need a moment to recuperate, so they sag against the building, gasping in the glorious clean air.

Mindful that someone is close behind them, Will scans the area for an exit. He hears the Thames lapping against the walls of the quay and sees the moon glinting off the water. Ahead is Tower Bridge. They need to cross it to get to St Paul's. There is a pathway along the river leading to the bridge, but it is too open, too exposed. They would be easy targets for whoever was following them.

He glances around. At the corner of the wharf building is a slit-like alley leading to the rear of Butler's Wharf. It might be a route to Tower Bridge Road. It is a risk and could take longer, but it would have the benefit of cover. It seems to be the best option.

'This way,' he commands.

They turn a corner into a street lined with walls and mounds of rubble, the bomb-ravaged remains of warehouses and offices for the once thriving docks.

'Keep going,' says Will. 'I will catch you up.'

'I'm staying with you,' says Sam.

Anna grabs Sam's hand. 'Come with me, Sam. Will won't be far behind.'

Sam looks up at both of them, unsure what he should do.

'Please, Sam,' says Will.

Sam nods his head. 'You better be quick,' he says.

'As quick as the wind,' says Will and watches them run off, hiding for cover among the scattered mounds of rubble.

He thinks again about the small soft hand from his memory, but his attention is diverted when he hears coughing and sees Wykes stumble into the alley. He is carrying a Browning pistol. He leans against the wall, clutching his chest and spitting onto the ground. Will keeps out of sight. He had hoped Wykes would follow the path up the river, but that would be too much luck to expect.

Wykes opens the Browning's magazine and looks inside. Then he searches his pockets once, twice, three times. He must be short of bullets. The Browning can hold thirteen rounds of ammunition. Wykes had fired a shot minutes back. That would mean he has twelve bullets, at most, remaining.

Wykes pushes the magazine back into place and looks up the alleyway.

Will darts out of view, but he knows he's been seen. He curses his stupidity.

'Is the bloke coming?' whispers Sam.

'Sam! What the hell are you doing here?'

'I couldn't leave you. This is my city, Will. We have to save it.'

Will sees Anna in the distance behind the cover of a burned-out car, looking back. Sam had obviously let her run on and doubled back.

Will peeks round and sees Wykes making his way toward the corner where they are hiding, but the smoke has slowed him, for the time being. Will darts back as a bullet flies from the Browning.

Eleven bullets remaining.

Will gathers up rocks and rubble. 'Get ready to run, Sam,' he says, stepping out from the corner and tossing the rocks hard at Wykes. Pain sears through his injured hand and up his arm. He shudders and steadies himself. Two of the rocks miss by inches but one connects with Wykes' knee. Will ducks behind the corner as Wykes fires again. Two bullets chip the brickwork above his head, spraying fragments of masonry into his face.

Nine bullets remaining.

Blinking the dust from his eyes, Will wipes his face and turns to Sam.

'Go!' he says and watches Sam run toward Anna, hopping dangerously over the rubble in the gloomy street. Will follows him and hears the crack of a third shot. A bullet whizzes past his ear and he tumbles to the ground, pulling Sam with him and rolling behind a pile of rocks.

Eight bullets remaining.

'Listen up, Sam. He's short of bullets. I'm sure of it. In a minute, we're going to make a run for it, but I'm going to try and make him use them up. After three I want you to run as fast as you have ever run in your life. Do you hear me?'

Sam nods. 'What about you?'

'I will try and distract him.'

Sam pales and clenches his fists.

Will peeks over the rubble and sees Wykes struggling across the uneven terrain. At least the destruction provided them some advantage.

He looks at Sam: 'After three. Remember, just keep running.'

Sam nods. 'Just keep running... just keep running,' he repeats.

'One... two... three!' Sam scurries off as Will stands up and tosses several more rocks at Wykes. To his relief, one strikes his shoulder with a satisfying thud.

Warm blood seeps through the bandage on Will's aching hand, but he ignores the pain and hurls two more rocks. Wykes stumbles back, raising his arm to stave them off, his face furious. He points the pistol at Will and squeezes the trigger. Will gasps and freezes.

But there is no crack and no bullet. Only a click.

Will and Wykes' eyes meet with a shared disbelief.

Wykes was down more bullets than Will could have hoped for. He wants to laugh, but he watches as Wykes begins to search his pockets frantically. He removes something from his pocket and smiles grimly. It is a bullet. Wykes' gaze fixes on Will as he puts the bullet slowly into the gun.

Will swears under his breath and runs, darting in between the shadows and rock piles.

The moon is high and the skies flash with the guns of war.

Sam is a short distance ahead, his little legs powering over the stones.

Tower Bridge comes into view through a gap in two half-demolished buildings. 'Keep running,' he calls to Sam and flies past the smaller boy. 'Faster Sam! Faster!'

Will's attention turns to rapid thuds and small clouds of dust that rise in quick succession at his feet.

Someone else is shooting at him.

He glances up at the bridge and swears the shots are coming from the top of it. Is it a sniper? He dives and rolls towards the burnt-out car and out of sight of the gunman's range. He turns, his stomach tightening at the sight of Sam who has not caught up.

Will beckons to him with both arms. 'Keep running, Sam,' he shouts. 'You're almost here!' And then, above the din, he hears an odd thudding noise like a tennis ball slamming hard against a wall. Sam stumbles backward.

'No!' cries Anna.

Confusion sweeps through Will like a grey cloud. Sam has stopped and sways on his feet, his arms limp. He looks so small amongst the decimated dock buildings. His eyes lock on to Will's and he smiles his lopsided smile. A small patch appears on his chest and begins to grow larger and larger.

Horror shakes Will from his confusion. He feels a choking worse than the black smoke. Trembling, he raises his hands to his temples and tries to scream, to cry out, but no sound comes from his mouth. Grief swells through his body.

Sam falls to his knees, his eyes never leaving Will's, and then the light, that had seemed so bright, leaves them forever.

Will can hear nothing but the blood pumping in his ears.

A figure looms over Sam's body. It is Wykes, smiling.

Will's grief crumbles like ash as rage sweeps through his every fibre.

'I'll kill you... I'll kill you all!' he cries and makes to run at Wykes, but Anna hauls him back, pulling him with all her strength.

'Not now, Will. Later,' she says, in hushed tones. Will resists, and cries out as her hand grips his softly.

In the distance, he hears the cries of the Londoners who had not quite made it to shelter. London would fall if he did not find the Stones. He has to do this for Sam and take his revenge later. A cold rationality grips him. Wykes is advancing toward them. Will turns and flees with Anna.

Chapter 37

Across Tower Bridge

Will's grief builds to a simmering fury that fuels his desire for revenge. He desperately wants to make the sniper, whoever he is, pay for what he has done to Sam. But that would have to wait. Right now, Wykes has one more bullet and Will is under no illusion whose name is on it.

They run from the ruins and out onto a main road. Will glances quickly around him. They are on Tower Bridge Road, he is sure of it. There is no one about. Cars and buses sit abandoned, parked haphazardly in the panic as people have scarpered, seeking shelter from the air raid.

Will has an idea. 'Look for a car with keys. Perhaps someone will have left them during the rush.'

Anna wastes no time and searches a row of nearby cars. Will takes another row, darting from car to car pulling open doors, peering inside and cursing his luck at finding nothing. Across the road is a bus with the driver door lying wide open.

Will glances behind him and sees Wykes' shadow appear from the ruins. 'Hide,' he hisses.

Anna rushes to the side of the road and out of sight.

Will runs to the bus, climbs up into the driver's seat and closes the door. He crouches down on the floor by the pedals and listens.

He can hear Wykes stepping cautiously up Tower Bridge Road, stopping

190

every now and then. Will does not move and tries to work out where he is. He is close, at the rear of bus, Will thinks. And then he feels the bus shift slightly as Wykes steps onto the rear platform.

Will holds his breath as Wykes walks up the aisle.

Will glances up at the small window separating the passenger and driver areas. He swallows. If Wykes takes one look through it, he is done for.

Wykes approaches. Will turns his head slowly and looks at the cabin door. He will spring at it and make his escape, if he has to.

Something clatters on the roof of the bus, and Wykes stops. Anna must have thrown something to divert his attention.

Wykes starts up the stairs. Will can hear his muffled tread upstairs and then a second clatter outside.

Another diversion.

Will feels the weight of the bus lean slightly to the right. He hears Wykes walk back down the aisle, down the stairs and onto the road.

His steps move away from the bus. Will's brow is damp with sweat. He thinks about Sam and fresh tears well in his eyes. He wipes them away with curled fists as a rage roars inside him like a furnace.

I will finish Wykes and Frost. All of them. I swear, Sam, I will do it.

Over the dashboard he sees Wykes hurrying towards the bridge. He must think he and Anna are on their way to St Paul's. Will waits a few more moments until Wykes is out of sight and pushes himself up. Something jabs against his shoulder. The key for the bus is still in the ignition. Sitting in the driver's seat, he places his hands on the immense steering wheel and thinks.

Can I drive something this size?

Outside, German bombers swarm the skies. What choice does he have? He looks back to where they have left Sam's body and, with a heaviness in his heart, he turns the key. The engine shudders and then shuts down. He tries again. This time the engine coughs and chokes three times before giving up. Will hears Anna climb on board.

'It might just be cold,' she says. 'Keep trying.'

Will tries again and the engine rumbles reluctantly. Behind him, in the distance, he hears gunfire and the screech of car brakes. He looks back and sees the old post-office van valiantly pursuing Dalton's Humber. He has no doubt Frost is in that car. They are heading towards the bridge. Will's pulse begins to race.

The bus engine rumbles, flattens and dies. Will grits his teeth and turns the key again. The engine coughs and trembles, stronger this time. 'Come on!' he shouts and, as if obeying his plea, the engine makes a clucking sound and the entire bus shakes into life.

'Well done, Will!' says Anna.

Will focuses on the controls, gripping the brake lever to his left and easing it down. He presses the accelerator with his foot and the bus rolls forward. The steering wheel is huge compared to the Embiricos and much harder to manoeuvre, especially with his sore and bloody hand. He slips the gear up to second, then third and picks up speed. Keep it steady, he tells himself over and over. Ignoring the blackout rule, Will switches on the lights. He cannot afford to lose time now by crashing into something he does not see. He presses the accelerator to the floor.

'Hold on!' he shouts.

Then straight ahead, Will catches sight of Wykes. He is signalling with a torch to the sniper at the top of the bridge. Wykes is standing on the middle of the bridge road, his pistol pointing at the bus. Will hears a creaking noise as if the bridge beneath them is moving. Behind Wykes, the bascules have started to rise. Will swallows. They are done for. He can see a smile forming on Wyke's face. He obviously signalled to the sniper to raise the bridge.

A surge of anger races through Will. This is not over yet.

'Anna, get down and hang on as tight as you can!' Will shouts.

'What are you doing?' she calls, but there is no time to explain.

He can't quite believe what he is about to do. But what option does he have? Wykes is aiming the revolver. Will can see his finger squeezing the trigger and ducks behind the wheel as the gunshot rings out. The windscreen shatters. Cool air fills the driver's cabin. The bus swerves but Will holds it firm and steers toward Wykes. There is a sudden look of dismay on the man's face. Will smiles. But then, Wykes runs at the bus, his stride long and strong, he leaps onto the bonnet.

With grim determination, Will mounts the rising bascule and speeds up.

Wykes clings on to the bonnet with one hand; the other claws at Will's face through the broken windscreen. With his heart pounding, Will leans away from Wykes as the bus hurtles toward the edge of the bascule and flies into the air.

There is calm; the bus makes no sound. A gentle wind fills the cabin, blowing through Will's hair and cooling his hot face. Wykes scrambles forward, but Will raises his fist and with all his strength launches it at the man's broad nose. He hears a satisfying crunch as Wykes' head rocks back. His grip loosens. He fights for purchase but it is too little, too late. He slides across the bonnet with nothing to grab hold of.

Will watches without regret, or remorse, as Wykes slips from the bonnet and falls, screaming. He sees Wykes' body slam against the edge of the bascule, silencing him as he plummets towards the dark waters of the Thames below.

With his heart in his mouth, Will grips the steering wheel firmly. The bus tilts forward to meet the other bascule that is now at a forty-five degree angle.

'Hang on, Anna!'

The bus slams into the bascule front wheels first. He hears a cry from the rear as metal scrapes against the road surface, sparks arch up the sides of the bus like fiery wings. The steering wheel spins to the right sliding through Will's sore and bloody hand. The bus swerves. Will pushes the brake pedal to the floor, but it feels like it is not working. He spins the wheel to the left as the bus mounts the pavement and crashes sideways against the steel barrier.

On his right, he sees the side of the bus peeling away. Ignoring the pain in his wounded hand, he hauls the steering wheel to the left while pumping the brakes. The bus swerves again, tilting left then right, the brakes screeching in protest. Will's strength is spent, his wounded palm is sweaty and bloody and losing traction against the steering wheel. The end of the bascule is ahead, the bridge flattens out, the bus jolting at the sudden change in angle. He pulls the handbrake lever with his good hand and the bus skids to the left, spinning three hundred and sixty degrees, the side panel flapping dangerously before finally coming loose and clattering behind them on the roadside.

With all his remaining strength, Will steadies the wheel, but the bus tips to the left, driving forward on two wheels.

Will throws his weight to the right in the desperate hope he can provide balance, but it is futile. The bus tilts further, he falls to the side of the cabin, banging his temple on the overhead control panel as the bus topples and crashes to the ground, glass shattering, sparks flying as it slides and scrapes to a stop near the bridge exit.

Will lies in a heap on the cabin's side, head spinning. The bus is creaking, protesting. For a moment he stares vacantly at the torrid flashing skies above. He is still alive but what about Anna?

He almost doesn't want to look but he hears her voice and peers into the rear of the bus.

Anna is gripping firmly on to a passenger seat, safe though understandably pale.

Still dizzy, Will massages his temples and looks at the bascule. It is up as high as it can go and shows no sign of lowering. He can hear gunfire from the top of the bridge. The sniper must be firing at Eoin. Fury grips Will and tears flood the back of his eyes. He will make that sniper pay. And then the bitter smell of diesel swamps the cabin, bringing him to his senses. A fire has started in the engine. Time to get out of here!

Chapter 38

London Crumbles

Will jumps over the driver's seat and pushes up the cabin door, which opens like a hatch. The sky is fraught with searchlights and droning bombers and rapid gunfire. He pulls himself up and stands on the side of the fallen bus. The left panel is missing and the passenger area is exposed. He clambers over the edge of the seats toward Anna.

'The engine is burning. We have to be quick,' he says.

He reaches down and pulls her up. They drop clumsily down the undercarriage to the ground below and give the engine a wide berth before running along the barriers and off the bridge.

An explosion rocks the ground.

Instinctively Will and Anna grab each other and turn to see the front of the bus in flames. They watch without saying anything, Will edging closer to Anna without realising. He feels her breath close. She is looking at him and he feels a warmth inside.

Something trembles in his blazer pocket. The astrolabe. He takes it out. It is glittering rapidly. 'We're getting closer,' he says.

'We should hurry,' says Anna, stepping back.

They sprint down to the waterside path towards the Tower of London, running breathlessly, their shoes clipping rapidly on the black cobbles. Will glances nervously back at the bridge. The bascules are still up and there is no sign of Eoin, or Dalton, on the other side. He looks behind and no one is following.

The flashing skies cast long flickering shadows of their tired bodies against the walls of the Tower of London. They are horribly exposed. One shot from the sniper could take either of them out.

Anna hides from view as Will turns up Water Lane and then glances up and down the wide expanse of Lower Thames Street to ensure there is no one suspicious approaching. When he is sure it is safe, he hurries across and hides in the shadows of a narrow exit road opposite. He glances around, waiting a moment, and then beckons Anna to follow.

They run through dark streets. The tall buildings obscure the moonlight and the glare of the searchlights, but not the terrifying rumble and boom of destruction that can be heard from every corner of the city. The ground quakes and the buildings shake as if they would collapse at any moment. Will wonders if this is what the end of the world would be like. Masonry dust and smoke fill the air, shrapnel falls from the skies, bouncing off roofs and walls and landing perilously close on three occasions.

Despite his determination and resolve, London is crumbling around him and he is frightened. Will begins to recognise the area and knows they are getting closer. The street ahead leads to a wider expanse, where looming tall in the sky is St Paul's dome, its great ball and cross silhouetted in the moonlight.

'What do we do when we get inside?' asks Anna.

'We find the eye. The eye will show us where to go.'

Chapter 39

The St Paul's Watch

Will and Anna crouch in the cemetery garden at the rear of St Paul's scanning the building for a side door. For a moment, it seems there is nothing, until a sliver of light shines from a gully at the side of the cathedral. It extinguishes as quickly as it appears. They hear the sound of slow footsteps, boots on stone, and the tune of someone whistling 'Wish me luck as you wave me goodbye'. It makes Will think of Aunty and the safe house, the last time he heard it. He steadies his breathing and slinks into the shadows beside Anna.

The whistler turns out to be an older man with a slight build who walks with a stoop and the stiff pace of someone who suffers from arthritis. He is dressed in an out-dated military uniform with a tin hat and a pair of binoculars around his neck. He is also carrying what seems to be a long spear, which is very odd. He does not appear to be a warden. Will wonders who he might be. The old man crosses through the courtyard and checks the cemetery garden, looking all the while in their direction. *Has he seen or heard them?* Will and Anna hold their breath and do not move an inch.

The sound of a bomber distracts the man. He fumbles around his neck and peers through the binoculars. He mumbles quietly under his breath then turns towards the front of the cathedral. Will and Anna exchange glances. They are both thinking the same thing. Will goes first, hurrying towards the gully and quickly down the steps. The door is unlocked and they both slip inside, closing it shut behind them.

It is dark and warm with a faint trace of incense in the air. Will takes out the torch and switches it on. The battery power is running low, the beam is fading but there is enough light to see they are in a wide and tall vaulted corridor made of stone. There are sconces on the walls and statues guarding numerous tombs. They are in the crypt. Will quickly gets a sense of his bearings and looks at Anna. He points west toward the front of the cathedral. Anna shakes her head and points north. Will shakes his head, defiantly, even though he has no idea how to get upstairs.

Maybe she is right. He relents and follows Anna through the unlit corridor, passing several more tombs along the way. It leads to a wide set of stone steps and a large gate. Anna runs up the steps and leaps gracefully onto the gate and over. Will joins her on the other side and they walk out on to the cathedral floor.

Will had forgotten how immense the cathedral is, more so now that they are the only people inside. It seems more an ancient stronghold than a place of worship and he has a sense the structure could magically protect them from the falling bombs. But he knows this is a fantasy. It is stone and mortar like any other building and would crumble in minutes if a bomb hit it.

He takes out the drawing of the cross, unfolds it and walks backwards toward the altar. Anna appears at his side and studies it with him. He looks across the vast space and turns the drawing of the cross over in his hands.

'I was right. It is definitely the cathedral floor plan.'

Anna points to the shaft. 'These are not jewels. They are benches and alcoves. But where is the eye?'

Will looks across at the rows of benches. In the centre of the cross should be something representing an eye. He walks to where the eye should be, looking down at the marble floor in front of the altar. It is then that he sees it.

'Anna, look!'

Anna stands beside him and looks down.

'Do you see it?'

'Yes!'

The marble design in the centre of the floor is almost like a giant's pupil. There is a brass grate like a dull golden iris forever peering upwards. Will and Anna follow its gaze and look up at the dome.

'Somewhere high up,' says Will.

'St Paul's has the highest point in London.'

Will swallows and rubs the back of his neck.

'What the devil are you two doing?' says a voice.

Will turns to see a stout man appear from behind the altar. He is wearing a monocle, a military cap and some sort of chain mail underneath his officer's jacket.

'Taking shelter from the air raid, sir,' says Will, saying the first thing that pops into his head.

The man walks toward them, frowning. 'How did you get in here?'

'There was a door…' says Anna.

'To the crypt,' adds Will.

The man regards them suspiciously and glances at the floor plan in Will's hand. His eyes narrow.

Time is running out.

'If you please, sir, I need to get up there,' says Will, pointing at the dome.

'Out of the question.'

Will and Anna glance at each other.

'Sir, please. I have very little time. I must get to the top of the dome.'

The man snorts, reaches into his pocket and takes out a notepad and pencil. 'What are your names?'

Will hears footsteps and turns to see the old soldier with the spear appear from the west doors at the front of the cathedral.

The man with the monocle looks up: 'What's going on Private Warby? These two…'

But there is someone else in the shadows, pointing a rifle at the old man's back. Will can see it is no ordinary rifle. It is an M1 Garand, semi-automatic. The kind of rifle used by a sniper.

Will freezes, his hands curl into fists. Who else could it be but the sniper from the bridge?

'Excuse me, Captain Snelling, sir,' says Private Warby.

'Private Warby, what in the blazes is going on here?'

Will interrupts. 'Captain Snelling, sir. That man behind Private Warby is a traitor and a murderer. He killed our friend.'

Captain Snelling looks at Will as if he is mad.

'I'm sorry, Captain. I didn't 'ave much of a choice,' says Warby. As they get nearer, Will sees the face of the sniper.

'You!' he says.

'Rupert?' says Anna.

Rupert Van Horne shoves Private Warby forward, his eyes darting nervously from Anna to Captain Snelling and back to Will. He is trembling, but his hands remain steady on the gun; his expression flickers unnaturally between psychotic and remorseful.

Will shakes with rage. 'You killed Sam, you bastard!'

'I should have killed you, too, and I will. Give me the notebook and whatever else you have in your pocket.'

'No!'

Horne turns the rifle towards Anna: 'Don't play games with me.'

Will steps in front of Anna and faces the barrel of the rifle, his eyes fixing on Horne's.

'You killed a boy, an innocent.'

'Shut up!'

'Why are you doing this, Horne? Why betray us all?'

Horne starts to laugh. 'Don't you recognize me, Starling? We know each other from years back. Four years to be precise. But, of course, apparently you have lost your memory. I don't believe that for one moment.'

'You're wrong. We have never met. I don't know you…'

'Liar!'

'Young man, please put down that gun,' says Snelling.

But Horne ignores him. 'Four years ago we were narrowed down to two candidates. We fought, you and I, with bare fists in front of them all.'

Horne's words are a trigger awakening a distant memory. The mists of

Will's mind part. He is in an underground room, putrid with stale sweat and cigarette smoke. Men are jeering and placing bets. Among them is a tall broad figure. Frost. Four bare-chested boys lie bloody on the ground. Two are unconscious, two are nursing their wounds. Will's knuckles are grazed and running toward him with a fast-flying bloodied fist is a younger Horne. Will snaps out of the memory, unsteady on his feet. He feels Anna's hand on his shoulder.

'Are you alright?'

Will nods.

'Frost chose you. Not me! You who came from nowhere!'

'Poor Horne. You really don't know what you are dealing with. You kill children and betray your country.'

'We are not betraying our country. We will be making it great again.'

Captain Snelling interrupts. 'I have heard enough. Put that gun away, sir. This is a house of worship not a battleground.'

'Captain Snelling, he is a traitorous swine,' says Will.

The Captain steps toward Horne. 'As head of the St Paul's Watch I command you…' but he does not finish his sentence. Horne's cold eyes stay on Will as he points the rifle at the captain and fires. The blast echoes through the cathedral.

Will turns to see the captain fall back onto the marble floor.

There is silence. Horne smiles.

Anna hurries to the captain and crouches beside him. Private Warby stands still and calm, his old eyes, watery and blue, flitting between the captain, Will and Horne.

'The girl is next,' says Horne.

Will feels his blood boil like oil.

'Warby…' says Snelling. He sounds weak, but he is alive.

'Yes, Captain.'

'Boer manoeuvre number seventeen, I think.'

'Good choice, Captain.'

Horne frowns and points the rifle at Warby, but the old man is surprisingly

201

fast for his age and arthritic bones. He swings the spear down so that the head smashes the knuckles of Horne's trigger hand. There is a crunching sound followed by a cry of pain as Horne drops the rifle. Warby swings the spear sideways against Horne's temple with a frightening force. Horne's eyes roll in his head as he falls to the ground. Will grabs the rifle and points it at him.

'Now, that takes me back,' says Warby, who stands over Horne with the tip of the spear nestling into the crook of his neck. 'Shall I finish him off, sir.'

'Good Lord, no,' says Snelling. 'Remember where you are. Is he conscious?'

'No, sir.'

'Then tie him up, Private.'

'Very good, sir.'

Anna helps the captain into a sitting position. His face is pale. There is a small hole in the chain mail by his left rib.

'We should get a doctor,' says Will.

'It's a graze. I'll live. Now, are you going to tell me what this is about?'

Will and Anna exchange glances. They both know they have to be honest, at least to some degree, one that would not make them sound like delusional fantasists.

'My name is Will Starling and this is Anna Wilder. Anna is an agent of the Secret Service and I am… ' Will stops.

What am I. Who am I?

'You see, there's this…'

'Bomb,' says Anna, getting in quick. Explaining mystical stones with the power to destroy them all might just be too much for him to swallow.

'Yes, a bomb, somewhere in London,' says Will.

'There are many bombs in London right now,' says the Captain.

'Not like this one. It's big, enormous, with the power to wipe out the city. That's why the Nazi's are bombing us. They know it is here. If they strike it, then it is all over. The war is lost.'

'Please, Captain Snelling. Will is telling the truth,' says Anna.

The Captain pauses momentarily. 'But why are you here?'

'Please, there is no time to explain. We must hurry.'

Another pause, Will feels his heart racing.

'The rifle, please,' says the Captain.

Will hesitates, but hands it across.

'Warby?'

'Sir,' replies Warby.

'Take these young people where they need to go. Access all areas.'

'Yes sir.'

'Thank you,' says Will.

'Go. I will keep an eye on the prisoner.'

Chapter 40

On Top of the World

'This way,' says Private Warby, gesturing to the staircase beyond the altar, but Will and Anna waste no time and rush ahead, taking the broad circular steps two, sometimes three, at a time.

At the second floor, the entrance to the Whispering Gallery, Will slows. It is dark and cavernous with occasional flashes of light from the warring skies above. He grips the smooth stone of the balcony wall, his eyes sweeping the gallery's wide circular expanse. A memory awakens, a voice from the past makes him falter.

'You must find your way to the top, and once you do, the Stones will find you.'

The voice belongs to Timothy Chittlock.

Private Warby arrives at top of the stairs. 'Blimey, this don't get any easier,' says the old soldier.

'Will?' says Anna, with a hint of concern in her voice.

'It's nothing,' says Will and crosses the gallery, exiting through to a narrow steep staircase, leading up to the Stone Gallery. They climb on quickly, reaching a doorway that leads to an iron staircase. The surrounding walls are tall and constructed from a solid white stone. They are at the base of the dome. Will pushes on climbing all the way to the top where he sees another door, the entrance to the balcony of the Golden Gallery. He pushes the door, but it is stiff. Anna joins him and together they give it one hard shove. The door flies open.

Cold air, smoke, droning bombers and the rapid ack ack ack of anti-aircraft gunfire flood his senses. Bombers and fighter planes seem almost within reaching distance. Across the capital, pockets of fire are raging. Clouds of black smoke hang over the city, which seems on the verge of collapse.

Will knows this is nothing compared to what could happen if a bomb struck the Stones. He looks up at the ball and cross, grandly silhouetted in the mercurial light of the full moon. Clouds are closing in, threatening to shroud its luminescence. He must move quickly – a clear night is needed for the astrolabe to show him where the Stones are.

'Help me find a way to the top,' he says.

They circle the balcony looking for somewhere to climb up. There is nothing.

Scaling the wall seems like the only option, but Will glances over the edge of the narrow balcony, and down past the roof of the dome. It is a long way to the bottom and he does not fancy his chances.

Private Warby arrives, puffing and panting, and holding his spear with both hands for support.

'Private Warby,' says Will, 'I need to get to the cross.'

If Warby is surprised at Will's request, he does not show it. 'Right ya be,' he says.

The old soldier looks to the top of gallery and focuses in on a spot between the pillars. He lifts his spear, pokes it around in the gloom and then smiles: 'Got it.' Lowering the spear to one side, he pulls down a narrow wooden ladder. 'That's all I use the ol' spear for these days. That and clearing off the debris from those bleedin' Nazi buggers,' he says, pointing to the skies. 'Now, the ladder will take you up to the ball where you will see a hole about the size of my thumb.' Private Warby shows Will his thumb to illustrate the point. He reaches into the side pocket of his old army jacket and takes out a large ring containing a dozen or more heavy-looking iron keys. He removes one and hands it to Will. 'Insert this key into the hole and push up. A hatch will open. Climb through and use the same key to open the second hatch on top. The cross has its own rungs on the north side.'

'Thank you, Private Warby,' says Will, taking the key and placing it in his pocket.

'Pleasure. Thank you for letting me apprehend the enemy once again. I never lost it, you know,' he says with a wink.

Will climbs the ladder, and Anna follows. He gazes beyond the balcony at the city below and feels his head spinning. It is so far down and, without the security of the balcony wall, his stomach lurches. Through the chaos in the skies, he hears Anna's voice.

'Don't look down, Will! Keep going.'

He closes his eyes for a moment and takes three deep breaths. Tightening his grip on the ladder, he pulls himself up, ignoring the pain in his injured hand. At the top of the gallery, he sees a fixed, curved iron ladder that runs over the domed roof and connects with a third ladder, which is painted gold and leads up to the great ball. Simple but ingenious camouflage, he thinks.

Buoyed by the great ball's close proximity, he clambers across the dome, ahead of Anna, and up the golden ladder, wincing at the cold wind that numbs his face and fingers. He sees the keyhole, and the faint square outline of the hatch door, and inserts the key, relieved to feel the faint tremor of the mechanism unlocking. The hatch door is stiff and heavy; it takes all his strength to push it up. Inside, it is pitch dark with the dry, dusty smell of age. There are layers of cobwebs, which drape his face, head and shoulders like a bridal veil.

He clambers up and brushes away the cobwebs. Something with too many legs crawls over his ear and across his face. In a moment of disgust and panic, he swipes it from his face. His grip on the ladder loosens and he slips down two rungs. He grabs the ladder, but the key slips from his grasp and falls into the gloom below.

Chapter 41

Oranges and Lemons

Horrified at his carelessness, Will listens as the key clatters against the ladder and then falls and slides down the side of the wall of the ball. He sees Anna just below the hatch door.

'Anna, watch out!' he shouts, hoping the heavy key does not hurt her.

Anna's hold on the ladder tightens and she looks up. 'What happened?'

'I stupidly dropped the key. Do you see it?'

'No. I heard it, though. It might still be inside.'

Holding the ladder with his good hand, he pulls the torch from his pocket with the other, flicks on the light and points the fading beam below. Anna is right. The key is still inside, but teetering on the edge of the hatch.

And then, a nearby explosion rocks the ground like an earthquake, the cathedral shakes and the ball trembles. Will gasps as the key wobbles, shifting closer to the opening, hanging half-on and half-off the edge. With his heart pounding, he inserts the torch into his mouth and scrambles down the ladder, the beam fixed securely on the key as if its light might magically stop it from falling.

He stretches his arm and reaches for it. It is a hair's breadth from his fingers. Leaning further in, his grip on the ladder is held by just two middle fingers to give him that extra bit of length. The key begins to tip over the edge. Wide-eyed and desperate, he lurches forward, but it tips over and falls.

'No!' he cries as the key falls, but Anna is fast and nimbly plucks it from the air. Their eyes meet for a moment.

His fingers ache from gripping the ladder but now he throws his weight back toward it, closing his eyes, relief sweeping over him. He climbs up to the top and is joined by Anna. They are so close, it is as if they are embracing. He watches her as she inserts the key and then together, they push open the second hatch.

A fierce gust of wind sweeps through the opening. He climbs through and helps Anna up.

They are standing on top of the ball at the base of the golden cross, which is almost as tall as a tree. Two enormous barrage balloons, like tethered leviathans of the skies, are floating above the cathedral. Around them they can see squadrons of Nazi bombers and Messerschmitts cramming London's skies. And putting up a valiant fight are the battling Hurricanes and Spitfires.

It is as if they have emerged into another world: one where they are small and insignificant, one that is perpetually dark and cold and filled with droning engines, rapid gunfire, whistling bombs and crackling flames.

He turns his focus to the cross and circles its base in search of the ladder leading to the top. He finds it on the north side, as Private Warby had said. Anna is first up, Will follows, climbing the golden rungs, and for a moment, he is reminded of a story told to him when he was young – the story of Jack climbing the beanstalk into the clouds. Someone read it to him once. Someone in another life, before all of this. Someone he can no longer remember. He swallows and pushes the distraction from his mind.

Ignoring the chaos in the skies around him, he reaches the top of the cross, which oddly resembles a giant flower made up of large golden petals.

Sticking close together they crawl across the top and then stand up in the centre. Will takes out the astrolabe, his pulse racing. It is not glowing as before.

'Why is it not working?' says Anna.

'I'm not sure.' He glances nervously up at the full moon, which is temporarily hidden by cloud and hears the thunderous roar of an engine. He turns to see a Messerschmitt flying past. He can see the pilot looking directly at him. Will meets his gaze as the plane flies wide and out of sight.

'Will, we have to hurry. I don't like the look of him,' says Anna.

Will focuses back on the astrolabe, waiting for something to happen. But nothing does. He frowns. Doubt begins to creep through him and he looks back at the moon, wishing he could shout and swear at the clouds, if only that would help shift them. But he doesn't need to. They part as if sensing his need.

And then the astrolabe's dull grey metal begins to glow and spark with miniature fireworks.

'At last!' says Anna.

Will's heart pounds as the lights grow in intensity. They spiral up and across his body and high into the sky. A cooling sensation flushes through him, causing him to forget everything and laugh.

He hears Anna's voice calling him. It sounds so far away, yet she is standing right in front of him, 'Will… Will… are you alright?'

'Yes!' he cries, his eyes wide with wonder, he holds the astrolabe high above his head, like the man on the mountain. The glowing becomes a rapid and bright flashing. And then, there is a muffled boom that tremors the air and for a few moments the torrid skies are gloriously lit with streaks of blue light that stretch across the entire city.

And then they are gone, as quickly as they came, and the sky is dark and full of danger. Will looks about, desperate for a sign or some sort of signal. But there is nothing, just darkness and flames.

And then he hears the mournful ringing of church bells. He isn't clear where it is coming from and scans the city, speaking out loud the old rhyme. Anna joins him.

'Oranges and lemons,

Say the bells of St Clement's…'

He looks in the direction of St Clement's but sees nothing. He is not sure what he is even looking for.

'…You owe me five farthings,

Say the bells of St Martin's…'

'When will you pay me?

Say the bells of Old Bailey.'

'When I grow rich,

Say the bells of Shoreditch.'

'When will that be?

Say the bells of Stepney…'

Will follows the order of churches but there does not seem to be any clue. And then he sees it.

'…I do not know,

Says the great bell of Bow.'

The great Bow bells of St Mary le Bow are ringing. He can see the church and its spire, at Cheapside just east of St Paul's. But there is something strange about the little church. Surrounding it, like something otherworldly, a blue light is forming like blue bees round a honeypot. It begins to extend upwards, shining like a beacon all the way to the sky.

'That's it!' he cries. 'That is where the Stones are hidden.'

'Watch out, Will,' shouts Anna, pulling him down.

He hears the rapid fire of a machine gun. Heading straight toward them is the Messerschmitt, its guns pointing and firing at the ball and cross. The bullets miss them, this time, but the Messerschmitt turns and circles back, stalking them like a shark.

Anna is running back to the ladder and gracefully swings over, out of harm's way.

A dozen bullets chip at the cross and one hits the astrolabe, shattering it into several pieces. One piece flies at Will's left cheekbone slicing through the skin to the bone. He cries out in pain and falls back against the giant petals dropping the remains of the ancient device. Warm sticky blood rolls down his cheek.

The Messerschmitt flies past and Will sees the pilot look at him with a grim smile. Once again the fighter plane turns sharply, its guns pointing directly at Will. This time, the pilot would not miss.

But Will is not yet finished. He sprints over the top of the cross, bullets pranging inches from his feet, and dives at the top rung, gripping it tightly with his good hand and swinging over the edge. He grunts as his body slams hard against the side of the cross, his ribs and left knee taking the biggest impact. His feet dangle in the air, his heart pounding; he dares not look down.

His body aches as the Messerschmitt roars furiously overhead. He scrabbles for purchase, hampered by the pain in his ribs and knee and his injured hand. He lowers himself quickly and carefully, trying his best to beat the next onslaught of bullets. They come quickly, crashing angrily over his head and hands as he reaches the top of ball. It is miracle he has not been hit.

He climbs down into the cover of the ball and waits for the Messerschmitt to pass. It flies by and he scrambles recklessly down and across the gallery roof.

'Hurry, Will!' It is Anna's voice. 'He's coming back!'

He climbs down to the balcony where Anna wraps her arms around him and squeezes so hard he winces. 'I thought… I thought… you were dead,' she says, her face buried in the crook of his neck.

'Ow… ow… I'm still here,' he says.

'Quickly, get inside!' says Private Warby, who is now holding a very old and long rifle and is aiming it at the oncoming fighter. Bullets rain on the gallery. Private Warby fires.

The bullets cease.

'Blimey, I think I hit him,' says Warby.

Will looks at the Messerschmitt. The pilot's window is cracked and the plane seems out of control. It is hurtling toward the gallery.

'Hurry!' shouts Will, as he and Anna run to the doorway. Private Warby drops the rifle and follows Will and Anna. Out of his peripheral vision Will sees the looming fighter plane. It is on its side, the wings slicing the air vertically. It passes feet from the Golden Gallery, its tail grazing the stone structure beneath their feet. The gallery trembles and they steady themselves on the balcony wall. The Messerschmitt tilts and glides across the rooftops below before crashing into a ball of fire somewhere near Blackfriars.

'Ha-ha!' shouts a jubilant Warby. 'I've still got it!'

'Mr Warby, thank you for everything,' says Will.

'For King and country,' shouts Warby, with a dramatic salute.

Chapter 42

St Mary le Bow

In spite of his aching ribs and sore knee, Will runs down the iron stairs. He can feel the skin around the wound on his cheek tighten as the blood congeals. He would have a scar there, for sure. He presses the drying wound with his fingers, the pain is hot, and causes his eyes to water.

They hurry through the Whispering Gallery and down to the cathedral floor. Will's eyes lock onto Horne's, who has regained consciousness. He is lying on his side, his bonds secured tightly around his wrists and ankles. On seeing Will, he scowls and says, 'You will never be free of them. They will hunt you down until they find you.'

Will says nothing for a moment. He thinks about Skipper, Violet, Aunty and, most of all, he thinks about Sam, the boy who had given him shelter when he needed it most, the boy who smiled and laughed at the oddest things, the boy who had formed a devotion to Will that had resulted in him losing his life. Cruelly murdered by the servants of VIPER. The fire in his belly twists and burns inside him.

'Let them come. I will be waiting,' he says.

Horne's face is red with fury. 'I will not go to prison, you know. My family have connections.'

'Then it will be easier for me to find you. Wait for me, Horne. One day we will meet again and I will not be so merciful.' Will surprises himself at the coldness of his warning.

Horne tries to wrestle himself free, but Captain Snelling jabs him with the rifle.

'Try any more of that I will put a bullet between your eyes,' he says.

Horne glares at him and settles down.

The Captain turns to Will: 'Get everything you need?'

'Yes, sir. Thank you.'

'Very good,' says the Captain. 'You look like you've been through the wars,' he adds.

'It's not over yet, sir,' says Will.

'Good luck to you.'

Will nods his thanks and turns to Anna, 'Ready?'

'Ready.'

Will looks up at the strange blue light, stretching up into the sky like a column. There are bombers circling it like carrion birds. His heart sinks.

'The bombers know where the Stones are,' says Anna.

'One direct hit and it's all over.'

They run toward the church.

'Where is the light coming from?' says Anna.

'The astrolabe is like some sort of mystical key that locates and activates the Stones. The Stones shine a light that can penetrate matter, like earth and stone. The light is like a signal, I suppose.'

'How do you know that?'

'I don't know. I just do.'

At the bottom of the church steps, Will stops and turns to Anna. 'There's still a chance for you to live, Anna. If you go now, you might just make it.'

Anna frowns. 'Do you really think you could have come this far without me? Sorry, Will, you might be some great super spy, but you are nothing on your own. Let's move on, shall we?'

Will is stuck for words and knows what Anna has said is true. With no time to argue, he hurries up the church steps and stretches his hand out to the blue haze. It feels cool, just like the astrolabe lights. He steps inside it and gasps. It feels like he is slipping through a shower of fire and ice, yet it neither burns him or freezes him. He shudders and stumbles through to the other side. Anna follows, trembling.

'Are you alright?' says Will.

'That was just weird.'

The interior of St Mary le Bow is small and unremarkable after the immense opulence of St Paul's. There is a stone font, and rows of wooden benches lead to an altar draped in a white cloth. The walls tremble and the water in the font ripples under a slow throb that seems to be coming from underneath the floor. Will looks down and sees a blue glow emanating from the gaps in the flagstones.

'There must be a crypt,' he says, glancing around for a doorway. 'See if you can find the entrance.'

They search every wall and corner of the church, running back and forth checking the same places over and over, but find nothing.

Will runs up the steps to the altar and looks around. 'There must be a way,' he says, hot and frustrated.

A faint waft of cool air brushes his face.

He frowns and looks in the direction it came from and sees the bottom of the altar cloth shifting slightly. He hurries toward it and pulls it up. Underneath the altar table is a flagstone with wider gaps than the others. 'I've found it!' he says.

Will takes out the screwdriver from his sleeve and uses it to leverage the flagstone up. Anna slides her fingers underneath and together they heave the stone up and push it across.

The blue light shines brightly below, lighting up what looks like a narrow stone corridor covered in cobwebs. Will lowers himself down, feet first and hangs mid-air. There is almost a two foot drop between his feet and the ground. He lets go, hoping to drop on his uninjured leg but that is easier in his mind, than in practice. He lands gracelessly, grunting at the shooting pains in his ribs and knee. He takes a deep breath and shuffles aside to allow Anna to follow him down.

'The floor's moving!' says Anna.

Will looks down and sees the surface of the ground shifting. Looking closer he can see spiders, bugs, and mice hurrying around them. They are crawling up the walls and through the hole and into the church above.

'They're running from the light,' says Will.

'This is all getting too strange,' says Anna.

Will leads the way towards the source of the light, turning around one corner then a second and third. They seem to be doubling back on themselves all the time, as if they are in a maze. He stops at the end of a corridor. Ahead is a cavernous square space. In its centre is a small building – a crypt within a crypt – that has seen better days. Its exterior walls are cracked and adorned with fierce stone gargoyles. A hazy blue light shines from their eyes and mouths, making them appear as if they are alive. There is a door made from heavy but rotten wood. It slides open with little effort.

Inside the crypt, the light is blinding. When Will's eyes adjust, he sees a round stone table on top of which are twelve magnificent jewels of different colours, all of which combine to form the brilliant blue beacon. He takes a deep breath.

It is the Stones of Fire.

Chapter 43

In the Midst of the Stones of Fire

'I was expecting something...bigger,' says Anna.

'Me too,' says Will, although the truth was he was not sure what he was expecting. Each of the Stones is the size of a large pebble. Combined in their original form, they would be the size of an ostrich egg, which on reflection might be big enough for a god of war, he thinks.

Suddenly, there is a thunderous clanging above them that causes Will and Anna to inch closer together. The walls start to shake and dust falls from the ceiling. It is as if the great bells have fallen on the church floor above.

'The bell's have stopped ringing,' says Anna.

'Let's gather the Stones and get out of here.' Will removes his blazer and lays it out flat on the stone table. Tentatively, he reaches for the Stones. They spark, crackle and spit as his hand draws close. He lifts the red one and holds his breath waiting for something to happen, but it just shimmers and throbs in his hands.

'It doesn't hurt.'

Slowly the light begins to fade, as if his touch as somehow calmed it down. They scoop the remaining Stones into the blazer and Will ties it up like a package. The brilliant beacon is no more. Instead the blazer looks like a glowing bundle of blue fire.

They hurry toward the crypt door, but Will spots movement in the shadows. He stops and grips Anna's forearm. He sees a sharp glint of blue reflect from a blade. He knows that blade. The knife bearer emerges from the dark, with a grubby, bloody bandage on one side of his face. His expression is grim, his one remaining eye fixed hard on Will.

The Pastor.

'It's over Pastor. Get out of our way.' says Will.

'The Stones will not leave this holy place,' says the Pastor, stepping into the crypt.

As if knowing what the other is thinking, Will and Anna separate, their eyes never leaving the Pastor.

Another booming explosion rocks the crypt. Cracks appear on the walls, dust and masonry fall around them.

'We will all die if we don't get out of here,' says Will, but the Pastor seems not to care. Is his plan for all of them to die here?

Will and Anna exchange glances as Will sets the Stones on the table. She knows they will have to deal with the Pastor together.

The Pastor speaks as if conducting a sermon. 'Ezekiel 28:14: You were an anointed guardian cherub. I placed you; you were on the holy mountain of God; in the midst of the Stones of Fire you walked…'

The Pastor's eye is opened wide, his expression grim and deranged.

'…I destroyed you, O guardian cherub, from amidst the Stones of Fire.' He rushes forward swiping his knife at Will but Will falls back just in time. He can hear the Stones throbbing with intensity, powered by the tension that fills the small crypt. He feels the room vibrating as a storm erupts around the Stones.

The ground and walls begin to shake with the combined force of the bombs and the power of the Stones. Will steadies himself against the crypt wall. But the Pastor looms forward, his glittering blade once again raised in the air.

'…I destroyed you, O guardian cherub, from amidst the Stones of Fire.'

Out of the corner of his eye Will sees Anna swing her leg upward with all the grace of a ballerina. Her foot connects with the Pastor's wrist causing it to bend backwards with a horrible crunch of bone. He cries out, drops the knife, and cradles his broken wrist. Fury lights up his face and he lunges at Anna's throat with his good hand. She punches and kicks him, but his grip is firm. Will runs at him, smashing his fist into the Pastor's damaged eye. The Pastor screams and lets go of Anna.

Will pulls her away and tucks the wrapped up Stones under his arm like a rugby ball. The walls of the crypt shake violently, the ceiling cracks and begins to fall down in clumps. Will swallows, hoping for one last piece of luck and, hand in hand with Anna, hurries out of the crypt.

He hears the Pastor cry out once more and looks back, but the crypt is crumbling and falling to pieces. He feels a cooling breeze and looks up to see the rim of the Bow bells peeking through a crack in the church floor. Beyond the Bow bells he can see the light of the moon shining radiantly in the sky. The ceiling creaks under the strain and the Bow bells crash through and hurtle toward the crypt, but Will and Anna are already running back through the crumbling walls of the maze.

Chapter 44

Return to the Wharf

Will and Anna sprint through the maze, leaping over rubble and dodging the collapsing walls. Dust and smoke fill the air in a dense, blinding fog making Will unsure if Anna is in front or behind him. He gropes his way forward, tripping over the uneven surface.

'Anna?' he calls.

'I'm here!'

She is somewhere ahead of him and he hurries forward. He hears other voices and then a firm hand grips his arm. He gasps and pulls away, thinking the Pastor has survived and followed him.

'Will?' says a voice through the din.

'Eoin!'

Eoin pulls him forward and shoves him gently ahead: 'Climb!'

Will cannot not see anything but leans forward and feels what he assumes is a large mound of rubble. He coughs, rubbing his stinging eyes and looks up. There are two torch lights pointing down and the sound of voices above him. He can hear Anna.

'There he is!' she says.

There are others, encouraging him on. He recognises their voices. It is Mr Singh and Eli Pike. Will climbs forward scrabbling for purchase and shifting his tired, sore body upward. He can feel Eoin close behind him.

The dust thins, the higher he climbs. A pair of hands grabs his arm and hauls him up.

'There ya go, Will, my lad,' says Eli Pike.

Will steadies himself against Eli.

'Thank you.'

'Lift your head up and I'll pour some water into those eyes,' says Eli.

Eli pours cold water over Will's face. He blinks and through his blurred vision he begins to see the bright full moon hanging over St Paul's. The skies are clear of bombers. They have left having failed to strike the Stones. London is saved.

Eoin is on his feet.

'Let's get everyone out of here quickly. There's an unexploded timer bomb down there and it's about to blow.'

Will looks back down at the pile of rubble he and Eoin have just climbed. What had been St Mary le Bow is now a smoking crater.

'It's lodged in the floor of the nave,' says Eoin. 'Everyone out, now!'

They turn and run from the disintegrating church back towards St Paul's where Will can see the old post-office van.

Eoin opens the rear doors.

Will hesitates. In the gloom he sees someone crouching in the corner, bound and gagged. He swallows. It is Colonel Frost.

'You caught him.'

'Aye lad. That I did.'

Eoin beckons them inside as Eli starts up the engine.

And then, the timer bomb explodes, rocking the ground beneath them. Will looks back in its direction. Clouds of dark smoke fill the streets like a heaving black monster. He shivers and feels a peculiar emptiness that he cannot quite explain.

They sit in grim silence as the old van trundles through the war -torn streets. Will can feel all eyes, except Frost's, looking at the bundle on his lap, which is no longer glowing, and seems like nothing more than some rocks wrapped up in his blazer.

He hands it across to Eoin.

For a moment, it seems the Irishman does not want them, but then he takes the bundle and Will feels an overwhelming weight lifting from his shoulders.

Frost is trying to speak through his gag. Will pulls it roughly from his mouth, curious to hear what he has to say.

Frost licks his lips and glares at Will with eyes full of hate.

'You think this is over?' he spits. 'You have crossed them and you will pay the price. You will all die, I can promise you…' But before he can finish Eoin's fist flies at Frost's face. Frost's eyes roll in his head and his body goes limp.

'I'm so bored with you,' says Eoin.

No one says anything.

Will hugs his knees and closes his eyes. He feels Anna's hand cover his and is grateful for her warmth.

The events of the past few days flash passed him and tears threaten.

'I want to go to Tower Bridge Road,' he says at last.

'Will, we need to get you to a doctor,' says Eoin.

Will shakes his head.

He can feel Eoin's probing gaze, but the Irishman does not object. 'Eli, take us back to Tower Bridge Road.'

Will walks passed the burnt out car, his stomach a pit of raw nerves. He can see the small form of Sam lying alone in the rubble where he had fallen earlier. He trembles inside and hesitates. He wants to call out his name but that would be pointless. Sam is gone. Dead, just like Skipper, Violet, Aunty and the others who got in the way.

He kneels by Sam's body, gently picks up his head and rests it on his knees, and carefully wipes the dust from his friend's eyes and face. Grief swells inside him. If he had tried better to protect him he would be alive today.

'I'm sorry Sam. I'm so sorry.'

Moments pass and a cold rage begins to grow inside him. Although he does not remember his parents he knows they are dead. He can feel it. That is why he has become the person he is. His muscles twist at the thought of all the other innocents who have died at the hands of VIPER or the Pastor. They are all monsters.

'This is all VIPER's doing, Sam. I'll make them pay for it, I swear I will. I promise I will hunt them down and when I find them, I will make them pay. I promise you Sam, I will make them pay!'

Will dips his head and fights back tears. He has battled through all of this without truly understanding who or what he is. He trembles and thinks of Skipper's friend who had gone mad after losing his memory and makes a promise to himself to never let that happen. At least not until he had his revenge. He looks up at Eoin who is watching him close by. He stares hard at the Irishman.

'Who am I?' he demands.

Chapter 45

Sleeper

Eoin instructed Eli to take them to St Ermin's, a Victorian redbrick mansion-block hotel in Westminster where the Secret Intelligence Service had annexed a number of floors and secretly went about the business of spying, code breaking and communication in the comfort of one of London's finest hotels. No one noticed the Service personnel. They moved amongst staff and clientele like ghosts.

Will had been looked over by a doctor and had his wounds treated, cleaned and dressed. Before his meeting with Eoin, he had requested some time to himself. He desperately wanted to know what Eoin had found out, but part of him was afraid of what he might hear. Was he alone in the world? Were his parents dead? He needed solitude right now to help prepare for whatever the Irishman had discovered.

Eoin had checked him into a room that was luxurious and grand, yet Will barely notices. He takes a long hot bath and washes away the dirt and dried blood from his skin; most of it his own but some of it the blood of his friends.

Someone had been into the room while he had bathed. Waiting for him on the bed are a new set of clothes: a red collarless shirt, blue tweed trousers with braces and a brand new navy blazer embossed with the golden Beaulieu crest. He is one of the Beaulieu elite now. A few days back he might have been pleased but now he is numb inside and feels nothing.

He dresses and hears a knock at the door.

He almost doesn't recognise her. Dressed in a flattering pale blue dress is Anna. Her hair is shiny, her lips are red and her eyelashes seem longer and darker.

'You look beautiful,' he says without even thinking.

She laughs and it lifts his mood.

They say nothing for a moment and then she steps forward and wraps her arms around him. He seems to float and pulls her close until he can smell the fine scented soap drifting on the surface of her smooth pale neck. He kisses it, feels her shiver and then finds her lips, where he becomes lost and, for a few glorious moments, forgets everything.

Later that evening Will is sitting at a desk opposite Eoin in one of the hotel rooms the Secret Service has taken over and converted into an office. Despite the events of the past few days and his reluctance to hear bad news, he cannot stop thinking about Anna. He wants to hold her and kiss her again, but that would have to wait.

'What will happen to the Stones?' he asks.

'They will be shipped abroad, possibly to the colonies, and buried in a very deep hole somewhere.'

'Someone will find them again.'

'Aye, I have no doubt. God willing that will not happen in our lifetime.'

'What about the Fellowship? They have a lot to answer for.'

'Yes, they do, and we will deal with them in due course.'

'Why was Tim in league with them? The Pastor was an evil man.'

'Yes, he was. Although one could argue that we are on the same side of the Fellowship. They are a society sworn to protect mystical and religious objects. However, their methods for doing that leave a lot to be desired. The Grandmaster and his cronies turn a blind eye to the Pastor's practices, believing what they do is for the greater good. As I say, we will deal with them.'

Against the odds, Will and Anna had escaped the collapse of St Mary Le Bow. Had the Pastor also managed to break free? Will felt a quiver in his stomach. No, he was dead. He had to be.

Sitting on top of the desk is a manila folder stamped CLASSIFIED. It is slim yet it sits there like the elephant in the room. Is this really the record of his life before he lost his memory?

'Are you ready?' asks Eoin.

Will nods.

'I went back to Tim Chittlock's house and found some files locked away in his basement. The news is not good, Will. I'm sorry.'

'Are my parents dead?'

'I'm afraid so. They were killed by VIPER and you would have been too had Tim not intervened and prevented you from going home that day.'

He rubs his arms and swallows. 'Why were they killed?'

'VIPER wanted something.'

'What could they possibly want that would require them to kill innocent people?'

'I'll come to that in a moment. Tim was a friend and colleague of your father's. They had much in common.'

'Was my father a spy?'

'Not quite. He was a scientist who worked for a research organisation called Teleken. They led the world in telekinetic research and believed certain people had the power to move objects with their minds. Unknown to your father, mother and Tim, Teleken was funded by VIPER. They had developed a drug, which they claimed could make a person telekinetic. It was a sensational claim at the time and people were queuing up to become part of the trial. Your mother was one of them.'

'Did it work... was my mother...?'

'No, the drug did not make anyone telekinetic. The research was dropped as was the funding. However, it was not a total disaster as your father discovered some years later. When your mother took the drug, she was not aware that she was pregnant.'

'Pregnant?'

Eoin picks up the file, removes a photograph and hands it across.

It is a shot of Will, smiling and happy, when he is perhaps eleven or twelve years old. But he is not the only person in the picture. He is holding someone's hand. He can almost feel it now, small, warm, with a firm grip as if it does not want to let go. He blinks and remembers the flashback when he held Anna's hand at Butler's Wharf only hours back. He stares at the picture. Smiling up at him is a little girl. Like him, she has thick dark hair. Will's stomach lurches. He recalls the dream he had on *The Outcast*: the one with him running away from the wolves to the safety of home where he found four graves. Two with coffins for his mum and dad; the other two were empty. He had thought nothing of it. It was just another confusing dream.

'In my dream, I saw four graves.'

'To the outside world the Starling family are dead, killed in a terrible accident. Tim saw to this to ensure you were not exposed.'

His mind swims and for the briefest of seconds a memory flashes through. He hears her laughing and calling his name and then he remembers.

'Rose…' he whispers, unable to take his eyes from the picture.

'Yes, you remember. She is your sister.'

From the recesses of his mind sparks of emotions ignite every fibre of his body – happiness long past, grief, and the one that feels so familiar to him now: rage. Rage at what he has lost. Rage at the murder of his parents. Rage at the kidnapping of his sister, his blood and the heart of the family. He trembles and feels nauseous.

'Through some quirk of nature, VIPER's telekinetic drug trial worked on your mother's new-born child, although they did not become aware of it until she was older.'

He searches the folds of his memory to find even a scrap of something that will help him recall any of his sister's telekinetic behaviour, but he finds nothing.

'Tim recruited you and primed you as a sleeper agent so that you could train, listen and learn about VIPER. He promised you your heart's desire if you helped bring them down. Do you remember what that was?'

He nods his head slowly. 'To find my sister.'

'That's right, but when Tim told you about the Stones and the danger they presented you diverted your attention to preventing VIPER from finding them. You did a most honourable and brave thing, Will. We cannot thank you enough.'

He is only half listening. 'Where is she?'

'First things first…'

'Where is she?' demands Will.

'Rose is being held in a VIPER stronghold known as the Red Tower.'

'I have to go there and bring her home.'

'Before we make any decisions you must understand you are still in danger. VIPER will not allow the indignity of losing the Stones of Fire to pass by without consequence. Also, in that head of yours lies VIPER intelligence that makes you valuable to us and a threat to them.'

'But I don't remember any of it.'

'But you are starting to. You've had flashbacks and you just remembered Rose's name.'

Will folds his arms. 'What do you want from me?'

'Let's do this my way. We will find your sister and we will tear down VIPER forever. But trust me, Will. Trust me and I promise I will make this happen.'

He can't stop thinking about what he has lost and the void it has left in his soul. His heart feels twisted and out of shape, its only desire is to rescue his sister and seek retribution for VIPER's crimes. If he has to he will bring them death and destruction. But Eoin is right, they cannot rush into this and Will knows he cannot do it alone. And Eoin cannot do it without him. For four years he was undercover, learning and waiting for his moment. He knows what he must do now. He will go back behind enemy lines, break them and destroy them.

Sleeper. Liberator. Executioner.

That's what he was. That is what they have all made him. He smiles, his destiny clear to him at long last.

ACKNOWLEDGEMENTS

I'd like to thank my partner, family and friends for their support, patience, love and humour. Without these pillars, *Sleeper* would not be published today.

Thank you, Rebecca Lloyd for your expert editorial advice. Every author needs writing buddies. Thank you Jean Levy and Olivia Kiernan for your encouragement, critiques and partnership on our many literary networking events.